The Fall of Two Houses

KEN HARROW

Dedicated to the humans dedicated to the craft of
writing, and keeping the arts decidedly human.

CHAPTER 1

CRUSHMA RAN DOWN THE STEEL corridors of his castle from the throne room, feeling something regurgitating through his stomach. The aches layered upon his aging body as he turned to his privy and coughed. Blood dripped from his lips as he went in the bowl, pushed a rune in, and water came out of a tube, with which he washed his beard. The bowl filled with water. Light shimmered from the burning torch which hung outside the window to keep the creepy Tendrils far away from his condition. Panting, he looked at his reflection in the ripples of the water.

Creases lined his face, and bags were underneath his eyes. His beard was thinning out, as was his hair with streaks of white and gray running through them. He coughed again, hurling into the bowl, splattering as his reflection was wiped clean. Sitting back down on the privy seat, he continued to pant until his strength filled his bones again, and in the silence of the few moments he was coming to terms with his condition.

I'm dying, he thought. As it plagued his mind, he looked up at the ceiling, realizing he was the Lord of the Throne. And he was certain with his age, the counts across the Westlands were plotting his replacement.

He needed to consummate an heir, and to do that was marriage into one of the other houses to add additional strength and embolden his legacy. Although, truth be told, his legacy was the least of his concerns. If he died and created a power vacuum, that would just give the Nezkas ample reason to invade their lands in his absence, what with the immediate civil war that would also take place as the various counts fought, and killed to become the next Lord of the West. His hands trembled before him as he knew this would happen should he not take active steps to ensure the wellbeing of his home after his death.

I need to arrange a wedding.

But Crushma wasn't a horrible lord. He'd like to think that whenever he could, he offered options to the counts rather than ultimatums. He took himself downstairs with an extra cloth, hurried outside to the courtyard. Large torches hung in the air signaling the dawn of the day, and he rushed past the busy activity of the nearest couriers making their way with metal slabs of letters to be delivered to various people across his fief. Going to the stable, which he then realized was a horrible idea as when he looked, he found his son Lorshmo, copulating with the livestock.

"By the Four Gods!" Crushma shouted, turning his eyes away but dashed forward, stifling a cough, before pushing his son away from the pig. "Pick up yer trousers!"

"Papa," Lorshmo said, pulling up his trousers as one of the stable hands took the pig away with a look of disgust on his face.

Crushma couldn't blame the stable hand for witnessing such a horrible act of human depravity, and he himself wanted nothing more than to strangle his one and only son for the reputation he has plagued his house with. There was no honor in bestiality. There should be no pleasure, There should be no courage. There should only be disease and shame.

"I shouldn't even be offering this to you boy, and in fact, if you weren't my *only* son, I would watch you hang from the gallows," Crushma swore, slapping his son across the face. "But you're going to be married soon."

"Papa." Lorshmo rubbed his face of the wound. A small trickle of blood dripped from a scratch. "Who would want to marry me?"

"Well if you didn't *pook* the damned livestock, people might be more inclined to take you up on your decrepit advances," Crushma snapped, and his son flinched. "And I wouldn't have to offer the entire lordship to anyone else. But choices are limited."

"But I likes it," Lorshmo whined.

"I don't care what ye likes." Crushma rolled his eyes. "You will either stop pooking the damned livestock, or do it out of sight. Either way, I must present you to the other counts who have eligible daughters. And you best not let this get out any further than it already has!"

Crushma scowled and slapped his son across the face again before bolting back into his castle to get to his office. With a large stack of clothes, he proceeded to write down his requests on them for a possible suitor. If his sons' affinity for animals and much less humans—*The Four Gods, even a Nezka would be preferable*—got out, there would be no one to take him, and no one to guide his son to Lordship of the Westlands. But all that to say, there were few counts that could be trusted with the land. Few of the many.

"Boy," he said to the courier who just came in from the door. "Take this to the post, and have them distributed. They are properly addressed but I need them delivered promptly!"

"Aye, Sire." The boy bowed and took the cloth scrolls in his arms and left.

The iron door slammed loudly behind the exit, just in time for it to be pushed open again. An armored man entered, panting. Crushma's eyes opened widely as he reached for his own sword as he stood up from behind the desk. He did not recognize the man who brazenly entered his domain without permission and no vetting. *Whoever let this man get this close to me is going to hang!*

"Speak plain and quickly," Crushma ordered, feeling a cough come. He reached for the cloth in his pocket. No one in this castle, even his closest friends, knew about his cough. They didn't know that his time was short and closing in on him faster than a guillotine.

"We received word," the man said, lifting his visor. "From the emissary from the Nezka horde. He demanded the release of the slaves."

"What is your name?"

"Jerkalta," he replied, and there was a tremble in his voice, as there should be for coming to the lord unannounced and unvetted. But Crushma was feeling particularly generous today.

"Jerkalta," Crushma repeated. "Tell me, which slaves is this emissary referring to?"

"The ones obtained from Morgsh Pocket."

"I see," he replied, and sheathed his sword. "Arrange for me to meet with him, and make arrangements for a catapult."

"A catapult?" Jerkalta tilted his head.

"Yes." Crushma peered outside the window. "It's to deliver the heads of the slaves he wants."

"Sire." The man bowed as Crushma turned around to see him off, and he bolted towards the door with the same urgency as he came in with.

"And Jerkalta, one more thing," Crushma said. "What is the name of the man who let you in here without proper summons?"

"It was Jethro, milord."

"Send him in," Crushma replied.

"Aye."

Finally alone in his room with the door slamming shut, Crushma coughed into his cloth and sat back down. As relieved as he was the encounter was short enough as to not affect his condition, trying to keep his condition private was a chore. The rumors had they gone out would only serve to encourage someone to prematurely come for his head. He tucked the cloth into an iron drawer. He filled his metal cup with water, and drank, and he felt refreshed before his next meeting with Jethro. Had it been something the lord wouldn't have been murdered for, he could overlook it and give him a warning. But Crushma could have been killed.

Jethro came into the room, escorted by two men. He was about a decade younger than the lord, and sweat beaded down on his face. Along with the bruising. Clearly, Jethro knew the fate before him, and tried to run away from it. But no one escapes consequences in the Land of Dreams. The man was set forcefully in front of him.

"Do you know why you are here?" Crushma asked, wanting the man's confirmation of his negligence.

"Nay, mu—milord," he stammered.

"You let someone here to give me news, a man I knew not," Crushma began. "That could have ended poorly had it been someone with ill intent."

"Milord—"

"You could have killed me, Jethro, and I will have no more part of your incompetence,"

"Milord, wait!"

"Hang him outside."

Jethro screamed as the two guards ripped him from the chair. The man pleaded with his life, but

Crushma only stared at him. He didn't care for the man who could have gotten him murdered and then escalated the Westlands downfall. Such men do not need to live within the Land of Dreams. *Dreams.* What was his dream? He pondered as the screaming lessened, and he was dragged out of the room. Even after the door shut, he could still hear the man's chronic wailing down the halls. He clicked his tongue, coughing again, but into a cloth so there would be no evidence of his condition.

He peered back out of the window. The orbs were shining brightly as he pondered his dreams. His wants and desires. The things that made him move and call him to action. The Westlands of the Land of Dreams were at risk. The potential power vacuum would bring it to a cataclysmic end as the Counts too drunk with power wouldn't see the Northlands and Southlands encroaching for a piece of the land to become their own. He couldn't have that. What with the Nezka kept encroaching upon Zer'kath's pocket, a historically contested piece of land which had mines, and a generous amount of Quesh'kal to be mined. He could see why the Northlands wanted it, but he had to keep his hold on it; if there was one thing he'd be remembered for, it was holding onto his grandfather's grounds rightfully taken. While he was sure the present Lord of the North didn't know it, Crushma's great grandfather had sacked Zer'kath's pocket sixty years ago.

Before he turned from the window, he saw Jethro brought up to a stand. Iron bars swayed as they pushed him up and tied a noose around his neck and lifted him up. A little delayed, but he would have much rather they struggle before they die. A swiftly snapped neck doesn't do anything to teach people the error of their ways. But seeing someone struggle, wriggling in the air as they cling for their life. It was effective. That's the image that keeps people on their toes, and in line so that they don't come for his head in the future, or to make sure they follow the necessary procedures and nearly kill the lord.

After careful deliberation and mediation, Crushma stepped out of his office and was accompanied by his personal guards as he made his way downstairs. May the Four Gods prohibit him from coughing in the presence of the emissary, for any sign of his weakness would be reason enough for them to cause a stir, and overreach their arms even further than Zer'kath. More chaos was brewing under his very nose, and he felt the threads of fate tying their notes, and he was at the epicenter of it all. In the midst of chaos. That was the lord's calling, and after doing this for twenty years it didn't get easier.

As he stepped outside he came to the ramp which he walked down with his guards on either side of him, wearing his fine clothes. A thinly threaded cloth, with leather patches. On those patches were drawings of his House emblem, which was a skull. The leather patches acted as decoration to his attire, but nothing more. A sword could still piece through if he wasn't careful, as the emissary, whom he saw at the bottom of the ramp, had their own protection. Not that a modest score of soldiers would protect a foreign diplomat here. The emissary couldn't get far, even out here. The only surety would be to brave the black abyss, but Crushma knew it was suicide unless one had an indefinite amount of Quesh'kal.

With each step he took, it was immediately apparent to him with the pain jolting up his spine how weak he'd become. But he bore it with a smile, hiding his true condition in the face of his enemy as he descended towards the bottom of the ramp. The Nezka was wearing a fine cloth, decorated with shapes embroidering inside with rocks to serve as something of a status. The Nezka seemed unarmed, as far as he could tell, but those leathery wings could still do some harm, even if they did have holes in them. Those holes, based on what he knew, is what prevented them from flying, and they were, all of them, born with the deformity. The horns pointed atop the creature's skull, parting its hair. As he got closer to the detestable thing, he realized his rage, and rightfully placed as such an imperfect creature stood upon his fief.

"It is an honor to finally meet you, renown Lord of the Westlands," the chief Nezka said. He was accompanied only by armed Nezka, with spears. Nothing more. Nothing less.

"And I you," Crushma fought back the vomit of his niceties. He hated these people and what they often did to his own kind of late. "I understand you want me to release some of our. . . guests."

"Hostages," the Nezka said as if to correct him, failing to introduce himself. "But yes, I was sent here by my lord to negotiate a price for their delivery."

"And where might you place them," Crushma said, motioning the ambassador to walk with him through the courtyard. As the two groups of people walked through the courtyard, he noticed it was fairly empty. He didn't doubt even his slaves would depart so urgently given the precedent he set during the last diplomatic attempt negotiated on his terms. Another Pocket of citizens were not released, and the humans of pocket Creshk were missing. To this day, he knew not what happened to the pocket under his care and within his territory. Knowing full well the dilemma that would lead to bloodshed, there was no real reason to give the ambassador what he wanted. "The pocket we took from them has been deserted with their absence."

"Might I remind you," the nameless ambassador hissed, turning his face only briefly as they walked over a bridge. Underneath the bridge was nothing of note. Crushma imagined many centuries ago, there may have been water running through it. "You went into our—"

"I encroached upon your pockets because you first encroached upon ours," Crushma snapped. "You take something of mine, I take something of yours. It really is that simple. Why should I give them back to you?"

"That Pocket is deserted because of your actions," the ambassador said sharply, but not rudely. "And I would appreciate it—"

"I would most appreciate it, Ambassador, if you recalled correctly the sequence of events that transpired the last time this happened," Crushma said, moving towards the lower regions of the Courtyard. Torches were lit now, for the shining orbs in the sky shed not their light down here.

"How do you mean," he saw the Nezka shudder.

"Oh, I merely mean to remind you that I sent an ambassador of my own, and he never made the return trip to inform me of the results of that diplomatic attempt." Crushma pointed a finger at him as the parties separated from one another.

The inner caverns in which they were now under was adorned with cloths draped with his house emblem. The sculptures of yellow metal were hewn together, and pressed against the walls underneath them. And under here was a veinwork of which he couldn't recognize. Blood spilled down here regularly, he knew, and Crushma had half a mind to kill the ambassador down here. But his wealth need not see needless violence. An ambassador for an ambassador.

"It was regrettable." The Nezka lowered his head to avoid his horns scraping against an iron work of an archway. "A mistake we don't mean to repeat."

"And my kingdom has yet to be paid for that particular kindness," Crushma growled. "And I don't mean to enact it upon you, don't you worry, but who would blame me if I did?"

"You are shrewd as a lord, one befitting your caliber of persuasion," the Nezka said after gaping his eyes. Clearly he now understood Crushma's ruthlessness.

"Flattery will get you impaled." Crushma waved his finger. "So, what do you Nezka scum have to offer in exchange for the 'hostages' as you so incorrectly claim?"

"We exchange a treaty of no encroachment for five years," the Nezka offered.

"You shouldn't have even bothered to come then as ye shouldn't be in our lands from the start," he snapped as his feet elevated towards a ramp that was leading them back outside. If he needed to murder a diplomat, outside this upcoming courtyard would be the place to do it. Away from prying eyes. "Do be better now, for my patience is wearing quite thin, and I have much better things to be doing for my people."

"I don't mean to intrude—"

"Intention or not." Crushma scowled as he took the first steps back outside under the cover of the green orb lights in the sky. His hand rested on his pommel. "You still intrude. Now, give me an offer I cannot refuse for your hostages, and then do with them what you will. A five-year peace isn't good enough!"

"We are prepared to offer an amount of money not to exceed three-thousand royal coins." The Nezka spoke sharply as if he sensed the walls closing in on him.

"Not good enough," Crushma sighed, his grip on his pommel relaxing. "But I am a reasonable man. I will take the treaty *and* the money and return the children back to you."

"And when can we expect them? Or should we take them now?"

"Nay," Crushma said. *I will catapult their heads to you.* "We will deliver them to you but first provide me the document that we may sign and be done with it."

"As you wish, milord," the Nezka bowed his head and departed with his guards.

He watched the company of Nezka go back down through his gallery to go retrieve the documents. He stepped into the courtyard, and sat in his cushioned seat, which he greatly needed his body to relax with such exertion. He hoped the Four Gods would provide some sustenance to his condition so the pain would not be as tremendous as of late. Sighing heavily, one of his servants was summoned and brought to him an inkwell, and he waited patiently for the Nezka to come back with the documents. And the ambassador didn't disappoint, for with such urgency were the documents produced and set.

Crushma signed the document after inspecting the print to make sure the details were all there. He grinned at the Ambassador before the cloth was rolled up, and he passed it to the Nezka who took it, and for a moment their hands touched. Crushma fought back the need to call for the creature's head. How dare he touch him? *Disgusting hands.* And soon, the Nezka fled to take the document back to the Northlands.

When they were out of earshot, Crushma said, "Prepare the delivery and align the guillotine. Make sure their parents are present."

CHAPTER 2

CRUSHMA SAT IN THE DIMNESS of his office, over-looking his fief as the green orbs began to fade, and the dreaded Abyss with all its tendrils came closer, diminishing his hope. The light faded, but the torches remained lit, and there was one flame in a metal cage swiveling in the wind outside the portal leading outside that kept the dark away. For here in the Land of Dreams, the most dangerous thing was not having weapons, but the darkness itself. Should he run out of Quesh'kal, the entire land would be devoured in a single day, and no one would hear from them again.

His mind went back to the letters he sent. It had been some weeks now since he'd sent the correspondence to see what interest he could get for Lorshmo, and thankfully, his depravity seemed to largely go unnoticed further than his fief. Though, his preference would be for his son to not engage in fornication with the swine, but here Lorshmo was. His eyes shifted as he read reports from the activities throughout the day. The children of the Nezka slaves had their heads cut off in front of their parents like he asked, and were transported in bags to be delivered by catapult to the Nezka lands. Jerkalta had been reassigned to door duty to make sure no one comes in unnoticed, and without permission.

But there was a knock on the door.

"Sire," Jerkalta's voice called from behind it. "The couriers have returned with responses."

"Come in," he demanded with his heart jolting with a hint of hope.

The man came into the room with scrolls in his arms and rushed to Crushma's desk. He could tell by the look of the man's face as he neatly placed the scrolls in an orderly fashioned, that he didn't want to be there. Crushma wondered now if there was some trap within the seals themselves as he looked on the pile of correspondents, but his reason and angst took over as he hovered his hand to the first scroll and inspected the wax seals to account for their authenticity. After inspecting all of them carefully, he was satisfied that there was no evidence of tampering.

He opened the first one and cut the seal. Unraveling it in his hands, he placed it firmly on the desk with his cloth weights so he could read it.

To the honorable Crushma,

I appreciate the offer for the extended marriage to my Ishbienne, but it has reached my ears that your son, whom you intend to marry, has very questionable appetites. I have not confirmed the validity of such rumors, but I do not intend to find out. Be the rumors what they are, I will not have my house associated even if they prove to be false.

I wish you the best fortune in your endeavors.

Sincerely yours,
Count Craft.

Crushma's eyes blinked when he finished the contents of the scroll. It was a terribly short letter but quite telling. Had he known the rumor already went out, he might have been more assertive in his letters to less request and more demand someone for his son. His heart was plagued with despair as he knew the task at hand was going to be harder than he could possibly imagine. But he couldn't blame Craft for the refusal, for had the positions been reversed, he too was likely to refuse. His bloodline was tainted by his son's depravity, and he wondered where exactly he went wrong in raising his son in this barren wasteland.

He clicked his tongue as he withdrew that scroll, and cut the seal of another one. A small skull with bones crossed behind it. A stylish insignia of grim proportions belonged to none other than Count Mala. He shuddered but his eyes gleaned with excitement, for as far as he knew, she didn't have children.

Just shy of thirty years, the woman was ambitious, but ambition alone wasn't enough reason to deny anyone. But he must first refrain from early judgments. Unraveling the scroll in his hands, he became accustomed to the feel, and the ink that decorated the page.

> *To the most honorable Lord Crushma of the Westlands,*
>
> *I trust this message finds you well and in the most amiable of moods, and I must congratulate you and your son on taking the next step in his life. Surely he must be proud in the interest he has garnered from you, for as you know in this world a good figure to step into the module of a teacher is hard to come by and not usually without a cost attached to it, much like puppets.*
> *I regret to remind you of my partner's premature departure from this world, and should you find yourself in the position where a decent, trustworthy suitor for your son cannot be found, I am quite available. And I will place my name in whatever contest you will*

have to decide who shall partner with Lorshmo.

Affectionately yours,
Count Mala.

"The Four Gods," he shook his head as he re-rolled the scroll and shoved it to the side.

The Audacity! Mala just lost her partner just a few fortnights ago and was already scheming to get into the royal family. His eyes shifted to the next scroll, but his hands trembled before he picked it up. He knew full well that Mala wouldn't have an interest in Lorshmo as a person, which was fine. This partnership was simply to be political to avoid the Westlands collapsing. The only problem with Mala as a suitor would be her escalating disaster. The Four Gods knew she would stab him, and his son before the marriage was fully consummated just to start a violent pursuit of the throne, and for what? Needless violence? The trouble with Mala was she was great when it came to starting armed conflicts, but poor when it came to ending them.

He looked at the insignia for the wax seal he was about to open. He remembered this one, and finger brushed over it gently. A group of razor thin wires decorating themselves with Grave Arcs. *Kira.* Before he cut the seal off, he tried to account for who was in Kira's house. His partner had passed some time ago, leaving behind a girl. Keneira was her name, as memory served. From what he remembered the girl was quite rebellious; however, she was already partnered to Kira's stableboy. Though a little infidelity never hurt anyone, he doubted the girl would be amenable to significant change, especially for someone like Lorshmo. If that was the case, he wondered precisely.

He opened the scroll.

> *To the most honorable Lord Crushma,*
>
> *May your enemies continue to fear you, and may you continue to find blessings in the abundance as delivered by the God Quda, and the prominence of the other three Gods that guide your path and your wisdom.*
>
> *I wish you the best luck in finding a suitor for your son, and should anyone else have been brought forth, might I appease your senses. Our houses have been close to each other, and I think it would be beneficial to both our children to continue our respective lines for all eternity. My eldest daughter, as you know is quite partnered and to get her to go along with tradition is difficult. An understatement. A much easier task would be to get a Nezka to tell the truth.*

I do have another daughter. Her name is Jera, and I would like to offer her hand. Should this be desirable to you, and we can unite our houses to ensure fairness to all the land and to avoid bloodshed, which I'm sure you're not wanting. And I would like to add that, should you have read any recent correspondence on the matter, you might not find someone willing to combine houses with you on account of your son's questionable habits. While not ideal, I will accept the beauty with the horrifying.

Sincerely yours,
Count Kira.

His hands trembled again. Out of fear of the rumors which were tarnishing his reputation. Of course this exists in the form of the rumor, but if anyone wanted proof, he had it ingrained in his mind and he couldn't unsee it. He had to assume them, Mala knew. Kira Knew. So far, both of these people were willing to combine houses with him despite knowing the rumors of his son's particular infatuation. His heart conflicted as he accepted the validity of the offers but no sane person or even reasonable person would partner with someone who had been found guilty of bestial copulation. *And who the pook is Jera?*

He pushed off the scrolls in question which left the offers on the table as he cut through the insignias from the rest of the Counts of the Westlands. Much to his dismay, as he frantically read through all of them, but not to his surprise he found they all denied his request and for the same reason. He could order it, but a house built upon an order, with no real passion or desire behind it was doomed to fail. Especially if one of the builders didn't want anything to do with the other. Such was simply asking for the temple of the Four Gods to collapse in on itself.

"Kira," Crushma said to himself. "This best not be questionable."

He wrote a correspondence to Kira and sent it out to arrange a meeting so he could properly attest if the relationship would be appropriate. But it was either this, or certain chaos. The courier left as Crushma was left wondering when the replay would come, and hopefully none of the other counts would allow any interference on such an important letter. His heart pulsed with anxiety over the coming fortnights as he waited and made arrangements for his detestable son to be educated on the matter of ruling and sound decisions. Of course, sound, wise, and ruling were words he never thought to associate his son with.

"But this is the life I had, the only one,"

Chapter 3

As he looked through the window as the days appeared to grow shorter with the inevitability of the winds of change, his heart grew heavier as his hopes for a smooth transition in his death began to fade. Fires burned out. As was he. Hearts. Passions. Loyalty. They all had their limits and now, and only now was Crushma faced with this reality as it came crashing down on him like iron weights on an old bridge. The green orbs in the sky lit to signal the coming of the day and the Abyss, and their horrifying tendrils receded. He never bothered to inquire what these large menacing things were. Just into the dark he knew there was certain death. He gazed down, and saw the fires being doused to preserve the precious Quesh'kal: the one thing preventing the Abyss from encroaching further into his territory, and his sanity.

His hope fluttered like the wings of a k'hara when the darkness lifted and beheld a lone rider. The man on the steed was strong and unmoved as he put himself forward. He rode light. There was only the essentials on his horse. The Message. The Messenger. The food to sustain the messenger. Crushma peered well past the horse as he saw the green orbs light up the sky over the road as it revealed more land. There were no Nezka, but a small detachment of soldiers bearing the insignia and banners with the same shaped appearance. Though he knew Kira wouldn't be far behind, he couldn't make out the details of who was being escorted as they hid the soon to be future mate of Lorshmo.

He hurried to the door after coughing and wiping blood from his chin. Turning himself to his personal privy and a bucket of water, he gazed at himself in the reflection of the shimmering light of candle sticks. His face was thinner. He pulled his lips back in a smile and he was missing some of his biters. He tilted his head yet again after washing his face and hurried down the stairs and ignored the pleas for his personal attention by other person inside his castle, which included other counts who made appointments of a personal business. He rushed out of the valve, and hurried down the stairs to meet the messenger, who panted as soon as he got off his horse, and his legs buckled to bow promptly.

"Forgive my appearance, Lord Crushma," the messenger said. "But we were quite delayed in coming here. A horde of Nezka happened on our pilgrimage, you understand, and has separated me from my company."

"Nezka," Crushma growled, barely audibly.

"But Count Kira is coming and well-armed still. He demanded I come with haste to ensure delivery of this message, 'I am coming soon'."

And I am glad to hear it." Crushma took the man's hand and eased him upwards. "Nezka do have a way with knives, don't they?"

"Aye," the man said, putting a cloth on his arm to nurse a wound. "That they do."

"And I will ensure you are well fed, and that you'll have rations on your return trip."

"Thank you, milord," he replied.

The messenger was escorted into his castle away from his presence as Crushma awaited Kira eagerly. Gazing down the road, he could not see the banners for his vantage point no longer gave him that luxury. The road parted his fief with stones on either sides of them, and it turned as the lanterns themselves were lit. But he couldn't see further as the path turned and it was covered under the darkness of the Abyss. His mind wandered at the gray black ceiling above him. It encased the world as far as he knew, and he wondered what lay beyond it. Not that he would ever live to see the curiosities beyond the Abyss. Creatures roamed there, and as his old teachers taught him when he was little, the Abyss is as old as the walls encasing the Land of Dreams. As he recalled this information, he ignored his moving environment from the creaking of wheels and wagons as they rode by. The scent of food he largely ignored as he waited for the answer that would confirm his hope for the Westlands. He gripped his chin to feel something, but even his sense of feeling appeared to be slipping away.

But when the clops of horses came by bearing the banner of Kira and his kin, his heart was elated and the senses of mortal being returned to him as the sounds and sensations became clearer to him. He felt jolted with enthusiasm as the horses came on with their riders. He heard the clamor of metal as his own body guards came from behind to protect him. But it mattered little if they were here or not for this was no coup. Or at least, Crushma didn't think so.

"Kira." He widened his eyes and opened his arms as he saw the Count plop off his horse with metal boots dropping in the mud. "Nice to see you, and I trust you've brought the suitor."

"Aye," Kira said with a great smile as he embraced the lord. "I wouldn't miss it. When you told me to send word I couldn't believe my eyes as I read your elegantly crafted letter."

"My apologies," Crushma kept his attention fixed on Kira as they conversed and the horses formed a circle, likely to prevent unwanted eyes from gawking at his daughter. "When you mentioned something of the matter I couldn't quite believe it. I thought you only ever had the one daughter."

"Aye." Kira nodded. "She is new, relatively new to the family."

"New?" Crushma frowned. "By what measure?"

"She hasn't caused a stir as much as Keneira has, which is why her name is spread throughout all the land, ye see," Kira explained. "But would you like to meet my Jera? Seems to be a waste of a trip without a proper meet and greet, yes?"

"Of course." Crushma's frown softened as he walked shoulder to shoulder with Kira and the horses parted their way and he could see who the suitor was.

She was a beautiful girl with a full head of hair. The gown she was wearing was slightly torn, likely due to the recent attack as reported by the messenger earlier. Her eyes glimmered in the nearby flamelight and it seemed like she was looking into the eyes of the Four Gods. So untouchable. She bowed at the direction of her father with a small curtsy, keeping the bottom of her gown clear from the dirt as she then greeted him and introduced herself to him. Perhaps, just perhaps she might be a dwarf? That would be preferable to the damnable thing that went on in his mind.

"Hi, Jera." He squatted down, and through determination stifled a cough. "Tell me, how many seasons have ye seen?"

"Only eight," she said.

His heart became conflicted but he dare not show it. This was in front of him now. He wanted to be done with the search or risk putting Mala in charge of everything. At the very least, children were easily molded. His hands trembled as he retracted his hand subtly from her as he considered the offer being made. A cojoining to the houses, but his detestable son will be at the whims of his own desires and when faced with the prospect of a child involved, there was something pulling at his heart, but he didn't understand what it was. But he knew what it was saying. In a loud voice inside his head that this offer was more detestable than his son's nasty habit of fornicating with the livestock. He clicked his tongue and turned to Kira who had a smile on his face, and Crushma wished Jera wasn't here or else he would rightly slap that smirk off his face.

"And what say you?"

"I say." Crushma took his friend's shoulder and turned him around. "I'll make sure you are fed, but let's talk further, shall we?"

"Of course," Kira replied with a touch of glee.

Crushma took Kira into his castle as the guards escorted Jera inside to the dining room where a small dinner was being served with him, Lorshmo, Kira, and Jera. There she would be safe from prying eyes, and with the servants being overwhelmingly busy, they wouldn't have the time or energy to entertain the gossip, or steal more than a glance. As he took Kira down the corridor, he led him up to some stairs which brought them both to his secluded study. Opening the door to it, a library was filled with scrolls behind a panel of glass. In front of that was his desk, and that was where he sat, knowing that there was a knife in his left handed drawer, should murder cross his mind.

"Kira." Crushma motioned for him to sit in the chair opposite to him, and so the Count did as the entrance of the room slammed shut. "What are you trying to do exactly?"

"Giving you an option," Kira said, inclining nonchalantly with a smug smile on his lips.

"An option to pair my son with your child who is not even ten yet, and certainly well below the proper age," Crushma snapped. "You can't be serious with this, can you?"

"But I am," Kira replied, leaning forward over the desk. "Yes, I understand she is quite too young for what we're proposing but that is hardly her decision is it?"

"I can scarcely believe my ears," Crushma said, and suddenly stabbing Kira seemed to be a desirable option. "My son is enough into his years and the implications—"

"Milord." Kira brought his voice down low, weaving his fingers. "When thee scroll came into my hands I wondered precisely what prompted this. I know this letter was scattered throughout the lands and every other count. I know that the contents of the letter was for a suitor rather than the typical ball one might host to find appropriate for a would-be-groom or bride. So, I've begun to think to myself why now of all times?"

"The world is changing," Crushma answered, hoping the condition of his nature hadn't gotten out if even by mere speculation. "We change with it."

"Yes it changes, but with the constant state of changes we find things are fundamentally the same, that is, in the midst of all our changes we are still the same as we were a hundred years ago," Kira said. "But the change isn't why you sent the letter, was it?"

Crushma remained silent for a moment before he considered answering the question as he pondered Kira's words. Why bring this up of all times, and why now? Surely there was a method to the madness as it sat unraveling before him. Like a carefully wrapped secret with the layers being peeled away and the unthinkable coming up to the surface. *Though I could simply hang Kira tonight.* And as that thought roamed through his head he heard a distant screeching and his blood ran cold.

"Speak plainly, and speak true,"

"I've only ever been true with you." Kira bowed his head, signifying his respect for the lord. "But you are not an old man, barely a few cycles older than me but I wonder if an illness has befallen you." At this, Crushma gasped, and Kira smiled. "I saw your cough, down there. I've seen it plague many men before me and the time is nigh for you to get your affairs in order, is it not?"

Crushma leaned back in his chair feeling another cough coming, but he wouldn't let the Count have the satisfaction of seeing him in such a frail state. A miserable man he had now become as he contemplated the machinations of the world that now bound him to Kira. To preserve his own line meant to join the two houses together, but he still couldn't in very good conscience give way to letting his son have his own way with a mere child. *But options are few.*

There is Mala.

"There is another one," Crushma said, though he didn't know how much longer he had. Was his honor worth waiting for?

"Don't be a fool, milord," Kira said. "Forgive my saying so, but if there was another option do you think the alternative was not equally depraved?"

Crushma could deny Mala's depravity for she wouldn't participate in the fornication of livestock. Nor would she implore the use of marrying children much too young for courting. Suddenly, the thought to stab Kira here seemed to be a poor option as the threads of his own personal conviction were slowly being cut away with the very unreasonable circumstances pressed before him, and he silently cursed the Four Gods which thrust this option before him. In the Land of Dreams, there were never good options. Just increasingly poor ones where the righteous and accursed are thrown into the crosshairs of such disasters..

Lorshmo, I wish you never were born.

"As much as I detest your heart and your own selfish ambition," Crushma leaned back with his hands woven across his chest. "And a conniving soul of yours knows where to push and I ask the Gods to curse you before the world's end for putting me up to this. I cannot deny you are the better option. May Jera be protected under my house until such a time as she grows older and able to defend herself from unwanted advances."

"Thank you, milord." Kira bowed his head. "You won't regret this.

"Kira left his seat and went downstairs where dinner would be served and rations then provided to them for the return trip home. Crushma felt a weight lift on his shoulders and then something resembling a hammer striking his ribs. While he achieved a goal of getting a suitor, and preparing the Westlands for a world without him in it, he couldn't shake the guilt of the last chink in the honor of his by permitting such a depraved marriage, especially considering the sake of Jera's father. Poor Jera. She was born in a world with a father who would sell her off to a brothel than receive the love she deserved.

He took his hands from the drawer and laid them on the desk before him. Shaking terribly so with the curse that filled his veins, even more so, that a man liked Kira lived while he was dying. That seemed to be the way of this world, and good people were often outlived by the depraved. Those conniving bastards who would sooner stab their friends in the back. Even more so that Kira ignored the curse Crushma wished upon him, but little did he comprehend at the time of the curse that a condemnation against Kira's house was equally condemning to his own house, now that they were destined to be intertwined by such horrid circumstances which, he was sure beget unforgivable consequences.

Crushma truly hated this world. Now with his son irredeemable, should the Land of Dreams burn to the ground someday. It wouldn't be its worse fate.

CHAPTER 4

KENEIRA SOAKED HERSELF IN A bath of hot water brought to a near boil as it touched her skin to clean off the muck and grime of her physical activities. Her muscles ached as if she was a victim of getting her arms and legs caught on the blunt end of an anvil and a careless blacksmith kept bashing her joints with his own hammer. But the water did good with her body as she relaxed in the metallic tub. Candles lit the room, and apart from the necessities, even with the amount of wealth she had, the room was mostly empty, devoid of décor.

Her mind wandered as she continued to clean herself as a vision of her now dead mother flashed before her mind. A frail woman with wires for hair, and a hollowed face. Eyes sunken in, and with a smile that simply read, 'I am happy' but with such an expression compelled upon such people it was harder trying to determine who they were lying to. Those around her? Or perhaps her mother herself. One day, perhaps, Keneira will find the answer hidden in the collective misery of every mortal being in the Land of Dreams, but alas, it was not to be this day that she would find hope.

Compelled then to bring about the rest of her day, she pulled herself out of the tub, and dressed herself before going through the hall. She knew her father would be coming back with Jera and hoped the Lord of the Westlands had any sense left in him to deny her father's fetishes of the unwanted. Tying her hair back, she removed the stopper from the bath, and the water filtered down into a basin below it, where she knew, or hoped it would be clean enough for the animals. The livestock were few this year, especially with the dehydration and lack of rain.

"Oh, what I wouldn't give for some acid rain, right about now," she muttered to herself as she made her way down the halls and smelled the scent of burning meat coming from the kitchen.

She hurried back to the eating hall where plates and utensils were set out, with iron goblets for drinking situated to the right of the plate, next to the spoon. She took her place, though empty the table was, at her mother's chair, and felt close with her again. *Mother, you died too soon.* And shortly after, her husband Baudet came by, smelling of dung. Though her nose didn't pick up on the usually abhorrent stench, she turned to him as he leaned in to kiss her, but alas, she grabbed his spoon and pressed it firmly upon his chest.

"Not like that ye won't." Keneira chuckled. "Go wash yerself up first. I expect Father will come home soon."

"How can ye tell?" He crinkled his nose, and pulled on his well-worn shirt.

"You smell." She pushed him further away as he chuckled. "Get back. Or else I'll knife ye."

"Ye'd dare not." He chuckled nervously.

"I most certainly would." She pulled back and reached for his knife, but retained her playful smile towards him. She saw a gleam in his eye, knowing he understood she was only playing around with him. "But I didn't say I wouldn't knife anything import-ant. Just things you don't need."

"Such as?" He tilted one side of his lips.

"Your fingers." She smirked. "Or yer nose. Ye don't seem to use that too often either."

"As ye wish," he retracted and laughed. "I shall wash up, and if fortune favors me in the least bit of these, I'll miss your father."

"Well, say a Prayer to Kreshkum then to main-tain what serenity you hope to keep in my house," she jested. "He still hasn't forgiven ye for stealing my heart."

"I'll make an offering." He bowed. "And ask that I can keep your heart intwined with mine.

"With what coin?"

"Yours, of course." He laughed as he walked out the door.

"Baudet!" she called, but a smile crept upon his lips in the silence. "That's my coin!"

He sauntered out of her presence.

***

She stood from her chair and went to the hole in the wall. It was an iron frame inside the stone as she looked downwards and beyond as the green orbs in the sky dimmed and the Fief below was lit with numerous torches and lanterns in response. The Castle's outer windows were always lit, and it kept the tendrils of the Abyss at bay, far away from her. But the monsters inside the Abyss always worried her, and she wondered if they were really worse than people. But her mind wandered as her gaze shifted to the road where plopping horses came with the wake of the banner of her House. Her father and Jera were riding and escorted through fief and she remained put, wondering if her wish came true. That Jera was fenced in and protected from the game of marriage.

Before long, both Jera and her father were at the dinner table, and it seemed that whatever prayer Baudet offered to Kreshkum, he managed to avoid her father, who would no doubt run ridicule against him, and her for once again defying customs and marrying outside what was traditional. She wouldn't accept a soulless count, or a knight. She wanted Baudet: a stableboy. Nothing more and nothing less. Of course, she would likely inherit the fief and all that was in it when her father finally passed but truth be told she had little interest in ruling over others. Much more so her younger sister's lot in life and she wondered if her actions pushed her sister into the politics of mating. If only to keep herself out of it.

Dinner was finally served and they, as a familial grouping, was left alone, save for the occasional chained and near naked slave to deliver more drinks, and serve more water. The roast came over, and the smell was soothing to her soul as it was delivered on a platter with a carving knife and fork already embedded into it. The calf was long, and seemingly stitched together carefully. Her mind wandered to it as she cut the meat into slivers before passing it to her sister, and then her father who had a look of tremendous disgust. But it wasn't directed at her.

"Human legs?" Kira gritted his teeth as he cut his portion up. The clatter of the silverware on the plate was enough to cause unease, and so it did to her own ears. "Keneira, why are we eating human legs?"

"Because the livestock aren't ready for the slaughter yet," she said. "It was your own rule, Father, that we don't kill animals for slaughter until they are dull and dry. None of our present animals fits the criteria."

"Loosen that criterion," he said, shivering as he chewed on human flesh. "Sooner rather than later for I have an announcement."

"Oh, by the Four Gods, please tell me no," Keneira said for she was conflicted of the game of marriage. She wanted no part in it, hence she married the lowly stableboy. But alas, that left her sister with the future. Keneira wanted her sister to grow up and fall in love and mate with the man or woman that fancied her, not be in some game. But was Keneira too selfish to allow herself some adultery? "Tell me the answer was no."

"It was a yes," Kira's eyes gleamed with excitement as he enjoyed the previously detestable meal. "It took some convincing on my end, but our houses are to be united."

"Father," Keneira stood up. "You cannot be serious about this? She's just a child."

"And ye damned well married a stable boy," he pointed a fork at her. "If ye had waited like ye were supposed to, and didn't marry the stable boy as I explicitly demanded you not to, Jera wouldn't be in this situation. Of course we could dissolve your marriage if ye want to take her place."

Keneira's jaw dropped at the suggestion. She could deny Baudet if she wanted to. But she didn't. She loved him, but wondered now if she loved him more than she loved her sister who sat close to her side. In many ways, she was like a mother to Jera in their mother's absence. There were no good options she felt. Nor was she willing to part with Baudet. Conflicted within herself, she placed her hands on her thighs, staying one with the cloth against her skin. Trying to find some grounding and perhaps there might be something else that could sway her father. If only she could think fast enough.

"I don't like him," Jera wept, drying tears with a washcloth.

"See," Keneira pointed, thankful that her sister providing some rationale for denying the lord this marriage. "Reason enough not to. She's only a child. Without—"

"Don't give me that! It is not her, or your choice to make. It is done. The ceremony will be in a few months," Kira snapped.

"Father—"

"I'm done talking about this, Ken," he replied softly. "It is done. And for the larger efforts to maintain sanity within the Westlands. If we don't do this, worse things will happen."

"I. . ." her voice trailed off.

Kira fired a glance at her to tell her to stop with the certainty that could only be a disapproving father's glare. A throb grew in her heart as she looked down at a crying Jera, and she crouched down with her, but offered no words of comfort. Her mind wandered with the situation, helpless as it was for her own actions didn't compel this, but rather, this was the price to pay to reside within the walls of the Land of Dreams. She knew there wasn't much she could do for Jera for there was no sensible place to run off to, save perhaps the Southlands. But her own comfort took hold of her for she knew finding work and food in a foreign land was exceptionally difficult. Jera wouldn't survive.

"The Southlands," Keneira said.

"What?" Kira tilted his head, baffled.

"I can take Jera to the Southlands—"

"Are you mad?" Kira slammed his fist on the table. "Abandon our fief? Abandon our tradition? Everything our ancestors worked so hard to achieve, you want to throw that all away? Keneira, is that it? We would be peasants at worst, merchants at best in the Southlands, assuming we even make it that far. The lord will find us and kill us! This is the only solution. I'm done talking about this."

"Fine." Keneira looked up at her father. "But I will be most vocal of my disapproval on this matter. You know this."

"That I do," Kira said, sipping from his goblet. "Go on. Shout it to the world. I don't care."

"I will,"

And shout she did over the next few weeks.

Chapter 5

MALA GLANCED OUT OF HER fief from this fine lovely morning, lit with the green orbs in the sky as men and women soldiers came marching back in with their patrols. The light of the armor shimmered with the sky orbs' illumination and she stood from her seat before making her way down to her administration office. Count Mala had a lot of work to do. Had she known running things was as tedious as it was, she never would have poisoned her husband. No. That's not quite true at all. She would do it anyway. Just a whim of a thought. Nothing more, and nothing less. Licking her teeth as she made it to her administration office, her trusted advisor, Gorlak, stood at the ready.

"Count Mala." He bowed lightly. "The dawn shines brightly."

"And brightly upon thee doth it shine." A sneer crept upon her lips as she looked at the mantel piece of her office. A recent discovery from one of their expeditions. A piece of metal with the coloring completely faded, but some engravings of what had been there before remained. Dents of material pressed against it, and shaped circular like a plate. "What news can you tell me of the Nezka front?"

"They're still holding fast, but it does appear they're mobilizing against Lord Crushma's fief," he replied.

"I hope he thought the land on the border was worth taking." Mala shook her head, and scoffed. "I swear. Crushma will be the death of us all."

"On that," Gorlak gravely replied. "I've no doubt."

"Count Mala, count Mala!" a Nezkama, a wing-less Nezka from the Eastlands, slave courier came bursting in. Her tunic near shreds, sweating profusely as her tail tucked between her legs like a mangy dog. Her horns twisted at the side of her head. "I've an urgent message for you."

Mala hissed at her and took the cloth from her hands. Unraveling it, she took it to her metal desk and observed the contents inside. The lord's signature was painted on it, and who could forget the swill's horrid handwriting in the runes of the common tongue. Inside was a wedding invitation. The lord's son, Lorshmo, was to be betrothed to Count Kira's youngest daughter. A disgusting pairing for more reasons than one. A gentle snarl curled itself upon her lips. She would have married him, had he not rejected her advances. But no. The poor little prince-ling was caught between a sleuth of limited choices of his own doing. Then the inkling of a thought. . . No, this was no thought, but a plan entered her mind.

"Gorlak, do you remember where Kira's Fief is?" she asked.

"Yes, I do," he replied.

"Leave us." She turned to the courier who dashed out the door, slamming the creaking iron hatch on her way out. "I'm taking my personal guard with me to his fief. I'm going to a wedding," kicking back in her chair, she grabbed a goblet which was filled with wine. "In two fortnights, you are going to order a tactical retreat. A section in the wall of defense must be breached, but keep it controlled. Permit the Nezka hoard to march right through to Kira's fief."

"And what of the citizenry between there and the front lines," Gorlak asked.

"Have the butchers ready. Preserve the meat, and you'll be rewarded with a feast." She cackled.

She thought to herself in her solitude as her attendants left her. Staring out the window, she remembered the rejection of the proposal she made and knew full well the extent in which Crushma tried to avoid combining houses with his son and herself. Likely out of fear that she would murder his son at his death and coronation of the new King. This was to be expected, and she remembered the name of the girl, Jera, who was Keneira's sister. She knew her well enough to understand the very nature of a man marrying a child must not have suited well for her personal tastes. Mala might have to alleviate that frustration.

Chapter 6

K ENEIRA STARED OUT TOWARD THE darkened skies, her sister clasping tightly to one hand while her spare hand weighed heavily on her opposite side. A chain she held, a ball of iron and glass, lights and smoldering embers inside, cackling, provided illumination. The cobblestones in front of her were the road toward the hunting grounds, some barrows, and an old cemetery Jera liked to visit, where their mother laid at rest. It had been three summers since her passing. As they walked the bare road, the green orbs in the sky shone. It was safe, for now at least, as she took her first steps forward. They'd be back, just in time for dinner. The servants were preparing several boars for the wedding festival.

It was not a wedding she approved of; her little sister, barely past eight summers herself, was to wed the disgusting Lorshmo, son of Crushma, Prince of the North. Rumor had it the lord himself went impotent, and the poor son, the bastard, was found early that morning balls deep in a damned hog, as if her father's brothels, which were offered the previous night, were subsequently refused for the sake of purity. Of course, copulating with animals was as clean as well water. She must admit, it was her own fault for marrying a low-born, but she loved him and wouldn't divorce him to save her sister. *Oh, gods.* To even think to have the same prick that defiled some hog inside her was *disgusting*; she nearly vomited at the thought. She contemplated taking Jera in the middle of the night before the wedding and ride as far south as they could. But what of the people in her father's fief? People she knew and loved? They would deal with the consequences of her actions. Hundreds if not thousands of lives in exchange for one. She wasn't so certain she was willing to commit to that.

"I want to see mummy," Jera said, her hand squeezing Keneira's, gently, as only she could. "Come, take me to mummy."

"Of course." Keneira smiled, looking at her sister with the flame lighting her face. Jera's hair was tied into a nice little bun, but her clothes were mournful to say the least; they just barely covered her shoulders. With a weakness about them, Keneira's hand tucked a few strands of hair behind her ears. "Just let me take care of the light."

She twisted the iron clasp at the top, opening a port with the glass, and embers danced inside the cage, emitting a little more flare. No telling really how much longer those orbs would stay lit, but as long as they did, when the Abyss would encroach upon them, this lantern would be the only thing either of them had to shield them from it, and the monsters that dwelt within. Yes, yes, the cemetery, too, was part of the Abyss, but with this lantern, they could traverse it safely, as safe as one ever dared. Keneira tightened her grip on her sister's hand and they stepped forward; the metal cage creaked with each step.

"Keneira," Jera spoke in her high-pitched voice, a shrill to it; unusual even for her. "What was it like?"

"What was what like?" Keneira asked, observing the road, seeing the break in the path rising upward, soil there was, and dying plants. *She is far too young for this.* She didn't want to answer this question.

"Marriage," Jera said. "What's it like?"

"Did father never tell you?" Keneira replied, leading her sister up the path ascending. She turned her head to look down at her sister, her brown braid brushed to the side of her shoulder covered in a green tunic. The eyes were innocent, gaping as if she herself was crying, not ready to face her future, not ready to continue on with tradition. No, her father already had one child who broke tradition, he needn't another.

"No," she answered. Keneira knew, her father was bastard enough to give her the responsibility for explaining these sensitive things. The bastard!

"It is a wonderful thing," she replied, drawing from her own experiences, which would not be Jera's lot in life. "Not without its difficulties, certainly." She gazed up to the sky. The air seemed lighter.

"But I don't want to leave and be too far from mummy and you," Jera said. The silence in the air was deafening, all things considered with the tantamount of responsibility being thrust on her shoulders.

"Listen, Jera." Keneira squatted down, the lantern chains scraping against the stones. What was she to tell her sister? That everything was going to be all right? No, that would be lying. Or—could she lie to her sister? Knowing the foul deeds Lorshmo was capable of? Her father was reasonable enough, but there was only so far his elbows could bend. And her marriage to the stableboy was enough of that. One of his offspring had to marry a count, or higher, and this fit the terms. The duty, to keep the house afloat. "Jera, sweet Jera, I know you're scared. But I'm here. What you're doing—"

What is being forced upon you.

"—is to ensure that our House will rise above the rest."

The house would already stand. I'll hold the status of a Count.

"He will hurt you," she spoke sternly.

The damned pig.

"He will like it, and you will accept it. Bear his children for the new generation."

Gods! She's just too young! And all for the sake of tradition!

"Come, let's go. I don't want to tarry anymore, so let's go find mother. Stay in the light!"

Others will benefit at her expense, even me.

Her sister looked to the ground in response. She didn't whimper or reject it, but simple accepted her fate, such as it was; or so that's what Keneira thought, wondering precisely what went on in that little head of hers. She was too young to understand all that was happening to her and all that was expected. She understood the concept of death, but not of love. Love was an idea that was too fleeting in the Land of Dreams.

"What's in the dark?" her sister asked. Too young and too sheltered was she from the opaque that such tragedies went amiss. Sometimes it was so easy to forget that she simply didn't know. How could she?

"Monsters," Keneira sighed, stepping upwards, taking her sister with her. "Careful, and quiet steps must we take."

They stepped forward. The path of the soil was soft and easy on their feet. The light from the green orbs faded as they drew farther from the path. The light from the lantern swayed, and the Abyss, like black smoke, swirled around them, trying to penetrate the shield of light it created, but to no avail.

Funny thing, really. Darkness cannot survive in the light, but this world had so little of it. The path brought them to a plateau, and the light shone on several stones, metal rods stuck into the ground, bones, and makeshift plants from a world forgotten and gifts from those whose dead were buried here. Save for one, and she walked Jera to it, the stone, a large one, a slate like a book. Upon it was inscribed the details of her mother; really, just her name: Mira, Countess of Morin, wife of Kira, mother to Keneira and Jera.

And underneath was written: *May the traditions guide you.* Her father had the statement commissioned to reflect a truth he wanted her to believe. Her mother wasn't one for traditions either.

"Here she is, but be careful," Keneira spoke solemnly, the lantern on the ground as she knelt, hands clasped over one another.

She silently prayed, but to which god, she knew not anymore. How could any god have wanted to create such a dark, pitiful place? None. For better, for worse, for good or evil, this world benefited no one, save for perhaps some sadistic lunatic who presumed the rest of the world was filled with masochists. Keneira decidedly was not one of them.

"Flowers!" Jera shrieked suddenly. "Keneira, we—we forgot to bring flowers!"

"Oh my…" Keneira turned to her. "You might be right. Go and grab some from the garden over there."

"Nothing e'er grows the'e!" she whined, voice wavering.

"Yes, but still, why don't you look? Or take a flower from one of the other graves. Those still work too, just *stay* in the light." Keneira heard Jera's steps scurry off as she continued to look at her mother's tombstone. Squatting down, her hand reached out to touch it, remembering what her mother looked like before she passed. A tear rolled down her cheek as she bowed her head. "I love you." She wept with the coming of the passing of time, lips trembling together. "I can't. I just can't. Baudet is here, but he is not you, and Jera, she looks so much like you, Mother. It hurts to look at her sometimes."

She missed her Mother. A good woman departed too soon from this world when a Nezka came in to assassinate her father but went into an unmarked room and brutally murdered her. It wasn't fair. This world. The things that happened to her and those around her. It was one of the reasons she didn't want to be Count. Too many things outside her control and people would come and attack her, and those she loved would likely perish before she did. But her mother didn't mind, while she was alive. The subtle conversations they had in the evening when no one thought they were doing anything. It was through her that Keneira sought the stableboy. She only wished she could have been there on the wedding day.

"Keneira!" her sister shrilled.

She turned her head, her braid whipping past her face. Her vision darted toward the garden: a pitiful display of flowers; there was nothing, save the black canvas behind it. *Damnit.* She stood and grabbed the lantern. Her blood pumped through her veins with each step, the light surrounded her, and she traversed the darkness of the Abyss. The light penetrated its hide, and the swirls of black smoke pushed back with the strength of the embers flaring from within their chamber.

Braving the dark, she felt the sludge creep into her boots. She grimaced and her heart pounded as the cold of the Abyss caressed her. *I shouldn't have lost sight of you.* She passed through into the unknown.

Mist drifted from her lips as she exhaled and pushed through the sludge, following her sister's voice.

"Jera!" she cried; the weight of the sludge attempted to pull her down. Each step was heavy, like a ball and chain tied to her feet, shackling her oppressively. Peering through the fog her breath made, as the dark touched the orb of light around her, she feared the worst.

"Keneira!" a voice shrieked suddenly. "Keneira!"

"Jera!" she called, a rasp in her voice, and she sprinted toward the sound, the swiveling lantern squeaked with the sudden jerk in the force she swung, and found her sister, the brave poor fool, dashing at her from the dark. "Jera!" she snapped, kneeling down, hands on her arms, nervously looking for markings of anything, bites, bleeding… nothing. The light of the lantern faded just a little as it rested on the sludge, the arms of the deep closing in on their spirits. "What did I say?"

"But I smelled—"

"It doesn't matter! You don't cross into the Abyss!" Keneira spoke harshly with a pointed finger.

"Why?" Jera exclaimed. "You do it all the time!"

To get away from—what am I running from? Keneira gasped, and that was all she could think. "It's dangerous. You don't know what's out there, and the Abyss can eat you," she reached forward, embracing her sister. "I'm sorry; I was scared. I didn't mean to frighten you."

"But Keneira," her sister spoke gently into her ear. "Come with me."

"We really should be getting back now. Did you find the flower for Mother's grave?" Keneira asked, standing; her eyes locked with her sister's innocent gaze.

"I found lots and lots and lots of things," Jera said, a smile curled upon her lips. Had it come from anyone else's mouth, she'd think she was up to something. "Come and see, you'll like them. You really will."

"Very well, but we mustn't stay for much longer. Hold my hand, and remember, stay in the light!"

"Yeah, yeah." Her sister brushed off the comment, taking her hand and pulling her along.

Keneira let her little sister lead her for a moment, the sludge still heavy, and the air grew thicker, and warmer for some reason she simply couldn't reconcile. The light illuminated the dark until they got to the mouth of a cave. Stalagmites and stalactites formed into a large ravenous mouth, and there seemed to be something fuzzy growing on the stony teeth. Her heart raced as her sister brought her closer to the cave. She couldn't have a nefarious mind. . .could she? Perish the thought, but onward she went, and the air grew warmer. Walking farther into the mouth of the cave; there was a large open space in the center, where she saw clear, streams of water. . . in *abundance*.

If her father knew about this he would be the richest Count in the land. But a thought entered her mind. Such a hidden pool of water in this great amount would lead all four lands coming upon them overnight, and they would shed so much blood to get to this water. It was safe from the acid rain that fell from the sky more often than not. And the water. . .it looked safe to drink adding to its value. She realized that they could have more land of nourishing farms where their animals would go healthy, like the crops, and they wouldn't have to resort to cannibalism or feed off of Nezka on occasion.

She didn't want her father to know about this. . .unless he already did; Kept it hidden and secret. She knew the consequences of wealth. Others with wealth would come for you. They will kill you, and hunt you down. Murder was all too common in the Land of Dreams, especially when it came to something as valuable as fresh water. Most liquids were transported to the *Sorcerer* who would then turn it to regular water.

With reckless abandon, she darted forward and her sister followed. Their giggles echoed off the walls as they came to the stream. The metal lantern creaked; the light still shining through its glass. At the stream, Keneira knelt down, cupped her hand, placed it in the cool water, brought it to her lips, and sighed in relief as the refreshing liquid poured down her gullet. She looked up and saw her sister walk through the stream into a clearing, where there was an artifact of some sort. A brown pole, thicker than a house, and vein-like shapes of itself crawled to the streams where the tips rested, digging themselves into the earth. Large things like those on the ground scraped the roof of the cave; some thick, some thin, all with green oval shaped bracts. They rustled as they lay above her, while other arms stretched down, hovering over another pedestal. She walked toward it with her sister, hating herself for trusting something like this so easily, but she was drawn to the artifact.

One of these arms stretched forward, branching out even, like little firm hands. The light from the lantern lit up an orb on which it lay, a red orb, with another brown stick at the top of it, and another bract. She took her hand, covered the bract, brought it to her face, and felt its firmness. Raising it to her nose, she sniffed it, but nothing caught her attention, so she opened her mouth and took a bite. Crunchy, hard, and… sweet. The white, pale flesh inside was moist. She took it to her sister. "Here, try it, it's tasty!" She'd never tasted anything like it before.

Her sister took it in her hands, and immediately Keneira wanted it back. She didn't know what it was, but it was delicious, more delicious than all the other dried fruit, meat, and various breads she ate every day. Even living with the safety of being heir to the Countess' seat, there were limitations to what was available. Her sister took the fruit and bit into it. A bright blush filled her cheeks, and smiling, she chewed the fruit, whatever it was, and walked toward the other side of the cavernous opening toward a little flower bed. Only these flowers were vibrant and healthy; not grey or black like those above.

Her sister was enthralled by one such flower and took it in her hands. The petals were bright yellow, with a large red center and a thick green stem.

Her sister discarded the fruit, and it rolled toward the stream. Keneira resented giving it to her, but her sister was precious, even if she didn't share the rest of the fruit with her. She'd never taste it again. But perhaps, now that she knew where this place was, could she come back? Yes, it wasn't a complete total waste. Jera plucked a flower with golden petals and she came to her sister, reaching up. "It's beautiful," she said, reaching up and tucking it behind her ear. "Like you."

"Well, aren't you the sweetest thing." Keneira fastened the flower behind her ear. "Did you find one acceptable for Mother?"

Jera looked at the garden again, plucked a purple flower, and presented it to her. "This one, it was the color of her eyes."

"Yes." Keneira smiled, taking it in her hand to inspect it and finding the purple hue to be like the color of her mother's eyes, confirming Jera's observation. "That will do just fine."

"For Mummy," her little sister said.

"Yes," Keneira repeated. "For Mummy."

Keneira considered Jera's innocence for a moment. She resembled a child. It only made sense after all, for she *was* a child. And yet, with the upcoming wedding, a nasty affair, she was forced to take on the role that should be left to adults. Hell, Keneira herself knew she wasn't completely considered an adult of sixteen seasons, but might as well be, with her father's subtle ailing condition. Such big things should be left to adults, or children at least capable of pulling a wagon.

They left the cave, but upon approaching the cemetery, Keneira peered back to where the cave was, the darkness swirling around it. Such a place, where the world was left with lack, with water in short supply, dying plants, or at least shortened lives… in that cave, life was abundant. She will come back here, if only to get some water. It wasn't terribly far from their land. She looked up at the sky. There was something inside that cave, giving nourishment to plants that existed outside the rest of the known, and bleak, world. In the distance, the faint green hue was beginning to fade. Night will fall soon.

"Jera." She knelt down. "We must be quick, for it's getting late. This flame can protect us, but only for so long."

"Very well," Jera spoke sharply, then scurried toward the grave site, tucked the flower by the stone atop which their mother lay, and retreated back to Keneira's side, ready to go.

Mother, I love you.

CHAPTER 7

AT LONG LAST, KENEIRA RETURNED her to the fief, but with heavy steps. Closer and closer to the fief, and nearer to the fate both of them dreaded. Inside her heart was her own inner turmoil with the prospect of a marriage she didn't approve of, but was unwilling to forsake Baudet, her husband, for her sake. Her own happiness was more important to her. She didn't want to live life without him, here in the Land of Dreams. Her sister could live happily under the lordship of the Westlands. Imagine that. *My younger sister is rising above me.*

The pathway was lit up by torches of burning Quesh'kal. Men and women walked with their dogs along the fief of her father with creaking lanterns at their sides. Over to the distance, there was a group of men and women by a great big fire drinking tankards of ale, slurring in their speech without a care in the world. The buildings around her were residential. Great big blocks of metal with windows and doors carved out of them. Further North of this bond fire, she saw the great spire of the Four Gods. Myriam, Kreskum, Quda, and Bruck. Four Gods for Four virtues: Fertility(laughable for the world was filled with famine and it wasn't a unique trait for the Westlands), Serenity(A hope that some people had, but with the disease, the famine, the murder, and constant wars over land claims, this was a virtue Keneira was confident no one would ever see), War(at least one of these Gods had their domains filled), and Scars.

As Keneira walked up the path as it tilted upwards, she felt her sister squeeze her hand.

"Can I go play?"

"Of course," Keneira smiled. "Just stay within the guard's sight, will you? And stay in the light!" She couldn't risk Jera thinking she could go into the Abyss without any form of protection. The Abyss… she didn't know all that was in it, except uncharted territory.

"Ken!" A hard, thick voice called out. She swiveled, and beheld a man in his thirties. Strong like an ox, he was. "Whe'e ye off to?"

"I was going to get changed 'fore the—"

"Stop it with that, plenty enough time later," Jorgan spoke harshly, arms crossed over his chest. "Can't let ye a'm rust up now, can we?"

"When ye start pronouncin' yer words correctly, I'll take these duels more seriously. But now? You want to duel now?" She broke eye contact with her battle-mentor(who had been mentoring her family for the last decade) from childhood and retreated a hand into her pocket; she didn't want people knowin' her stance was still weak when wielding her sword. A little kick to the thigh would send her tumbling.

"Just 'round the road. As yer mentor, I train in the art of sword play, not werds," he replied, as he led her to a dueling circle. "Ya ca'ied yer sword with ye, did ye not?"

"Did ye bothe' ta look?" she said, her hand on the pommel of her blade. She wished she'd had the time to set her crossbow down somewhere; it was heavy with the iron stock attached to it. Sturdy thing, that.

"Yes, well, as heir to the countess' seat, you must be prepared and disciplined," he said to her, once they were well away from everyone's sight. "Didn't want to publicly disgrace ye, now, we best start workin' on that stance."

He was right, of course; even a countess was fated to fight should the occasion call for it, and there were no shortage of occasions with the Eastlands. The brutish Nezkama threatened discourse on their flank all the time. The men to the south rarely came to their aid, unless they could raid and pillage and rape the women for hazard reward. Griping, she stood, drew her sword, and put two hands on her hilt. Her back leg bent, ready to pivot, but kept her front leg still twisted at the ankle, more than half her body weight leaned on the hind.

"Steady that stance!" he said, and pointed. "Hold that blade tightly. Tighter, I said!"

"This is my tightest grip, ye bastard!" she swore.

"Ha!" He swung his sword at her. Tilting her body, she parried the blade, but the force of the strike pushed her off balance. "If that is the tightest grip you can muster, I'd hate to see the sorry fate your house will have. After all, yer the only one who can wield a sword. Poor little Jera is far too young."

"Too young! Poor baby girl," she said, swiveling her feet and swinging her sword at him, attempting to nick his finger. He retracted his strike, and kicked the end of her sword. "Who will ever come to her aid?"

"Well…" He thrust his sword at her, and, completely exposed, it grazed her neck. She ducked down, twisted her body, and danced on her feet away from his reach. "Not that you'll have to worry about that much, tradition and all."

"She's too young, Jorgan." She spoke, knowing he referred to the comfortable life behind the protection of the lord's men. "Far too young to be given in marriage."

"Yes." He scratched his head, sheathing his sword. She did the same. "I think that's enough for today; your stance is improving."

"Thank you," she said, bowing briefly in respect.

"Not much we can do about tradition," he said. "I agree, but tradition is tradition, what with the rumors of the lord and prince being true. Since none of the other counts offered their own offspring for it, the lack of a lord would put our land into chaos. It's almost like they wanted this."

"Why?" she asked. "My father is the head count—"

"Head count or not, doesn't matter, whatever the lord says, he does," he snapped. "Keneira, you must discard your own morality, you might learn somethin'. There is no right, no wrong; there is just what is. The soonah you learn this, the soonah you will accept it. Accept it, or else all will fall into chaos."

"And for you, what is, just is?" she asked. This was a rather short sparring match, did her swordplay partner just decide it was time for a good lecturing?

"Just. Just is. Justice," he grunted. "Traditions were set in stone, and they ought not be uprooted like pointless weeds. Keneira, you know too well that my fate is tied to the house. The house survives, so do I. Justice," he growled. "Is a mere word. There is nothing just in this world. Get used to it."

"What?" she exclaimed. "But what are our traditions that we s—"

"Your mother believed in our traditions, in our customs," he said. Keneira remembered the engraving on her mother's tombstone. "Who are you to deny them? We don't get to decide what they are. Trust me when I say—"

"No, Jorgan!" she snapped. "What are traditions but man-made constructs?"

"And what are you going to do?" he growled. It was more a statement than a question. One of several in which he had asked in the past, to stop her passion, to force a moment of logic within her. It worked every time. What would she do? Nothing.

That's what. She'd see her little sister off, married to that pig pookin' bastard! Removed from their house, to inherit the lordship, while she was left with the countship and her lowborn husband. There was nothing she would do, or else risk the wrath of the lord and face his justice by way of public hanging. The spectators would dance, seeing her body swing on the rope, gasping for breath.

"I don't know," she finally stammered.

"Good," he said. "Then nothing is what you should do." He finally sighed, taking a seat upon a rock. "Young as she is, it would be most unwise to deny the will of the lord. The prince, less than reasonable."

"I understand," she said.

"Good, see to it that you do," he replied, then stood and proceeded to walk toward one path leading to the butchery.

CHAPTER 8

THE IRON WALLS ECHOED WITH various foot-steps. Golden hue of flamelight from candles layered across the grand hall. Loud conversations echoed through all corners of the room. Food there was, aplenty, for the lord provided for the feast, and her father, Kira, provided the venue and the servants who would cook and prepare the food. The music played on leather instruments with strings made from horse hair.

Keneira ate a turkey leg from her plate. A boar roasted in front of her as she looked across the hall. Her father and Lord Crushma spoke to one another, laughing like lifelong friends, but she knew the purpose of such niceties was always political. The only thing she could understand was the laughter, and to their side, the future betrothed, Lorshmo and Jera sitting at the lord's right-hand. The dreadful prince was already intertwining his filthy little fingers in her hair, laughing as his future bride looked away, keeping herself busy, occupied and distracted with the plate of grey lettuce on her plate. Her hands trembled as Lorshmo wrapped his arm around her sister's shoulders.

"Try not to think on it too much," Baudet said at Keneira's side, reaching in and pecking her on the cheek. He scraped the plate with his eating utensils.

"Dravel, dravel, dravel!" she growled. "Dare I say you don't understand." And why would he? He wasn't highborn like her. Perhaps she did in fact marry poorly. No. Objectively speaking, she did, all in the sake of adoration, for love's sake. Perhaps her decision to throw tradition on the dung heap led to her sister slowly being groomed to mate with whatever that *thing* was. Only a *thing* would dare pook a pig. "You wouldn't understand. Leave it alone."

"I can't leave it alone," he said, turning to her, brushing a strand of hair behind her ear. "You'll take it out on me later, and for once since this sta'ted, I'd like a good night's sleep."

"When have I ever taken out my problems on you?" she asked, appreciating the warmth of his hand against her flesh. "I love you. You know that."

"As do I, and I know you love me." His hand touched her chin, tilting her gaze up. "But you do it every day. Perhaps you forget I'm lowborn, a stable boy, that's all I ever was, but when I caught such infatuation from you, I couldn't help but pursue you." He gulped down the rest of his ale. "Speaking of which, I've horses to feed now. Try not to do anything rash, will you?"

She shook her head, kissing him firmly on the lips as he left. The chair moved, and he disappeared behind the crowd of people, and in the center of the room, people started to dance. Perhaps, when she was countess, she could enjoy a dance with the stable boy, her husband. Lorshmo took her sister's hand and onto the dance floor. Of course, with the promise of tomorrow, Jera couldn't very well deny such a gesture. He stroked her hair, the hair Keneira braided, and who knew if the dirty little bastard at least brushed his hands through some water first before touching her. Gritting her teeth, Keneira took a draught of ale.

"Poor dear, your husband seemed to abandon you before the dance," a voice called, and she turned. A strong, red-headed woman in a lovely dress was looking at her with sympathy. "Dare I keep you company? Or will you push me away?"

"By all means, Count Mala," she motioned to the empty seat beside her. "Take a seat; it has since become available."

"I see," Mala elegantly sat next to her. "Dreadful; I must say, a girl as young as yourself should be out dancing. Such a shame he left."

"Well, he is a stableboy," she said. "Father doesn't approve of him."

"No," Mala replied, taking a sip of her ale which she had brought with her. "No doubt. A little strong about the shoulders, though; you certainly know how to choose the right stock."

"We're not livestock, Mala." Keneira frowned. "Treat my husband with some dignity. He gets enough of that from my father; he doesn't need it from you, too."

"Sorry to suggest any disrespect," Mala apologized. "Milady."

"Nothing to forgive," she permitted herself to smile as she turned her gaze back to her sister, and her face betrayed her disgust she had for the lord. She felt her teeth grinding.

"Milady," Mala said, her hand stretching forward, clasping atop Keneira's with an iron grip. "Might I have your ear a moment?"

"Yes, Count Mala." She swiveled over to her, putting her hand atop Mala's. She had to admit, the countess' grip was tighter than she expected. "What words, pray tell, do you have to infect my ear with?"

"Oh, what's court life without a little friendly gossip?" she sneered, bending forward. "You see, I have it quite on good authority, dear, that you do not approve of this marriage."

"No," she replied, shifting her gaze from her. "But that's hardly a surprise, I am quite vocal on the matter."

"Except now," Mala replied. "Think not that I wasn't listening to your quarrel with your beloved."

"She's too young, Mala," she said. "Too young."

"She's too young, but he's not that old; perhaps just a few years older than you," she said, finger to her lips. "Marrying young, especially for such political gain, is not out of our customs. Your father is certainly no fool."

"To hell with our customs!" she whispered sharply. "To hell with them all!"

"To that," Mala drank. "You and I are in quite the agreement. Such drivel. What those of the lesser stock than you and I understand, is if you understand customs and traditions, you can make them say whatever it is you want them to say. Things change, so do our twists on the old lore goes, to fit our needs. I didn't rise to my station by merely following tradition. Now, look at me, a count, not a mere countess. When you come into the seat when your father dies, you can make it that your stableboy is the countess, and you the count."

"And what did you do to make yourself the count?" Keneira took the ale to her lips, poised to take a sip, and slid her chair closer to Mala. "Surely there was a more complicated solution to your individual disposition."

"I killed him," she answered with a smile, as ale slipped down her lips, this seemed to her, not an unusual thing Mala would suggest. Keneira coughed. "The count, that is. After a night of enthusiastic love making, I poisoned his morning ale. It was beautiful."

"The Four Gods," she wiped the ale and spit from her chin with a cloth. "You're bold to admit that to me. What's to say I don't—"

"Hush now," Mala replied, two fingers pressed to her lips. "We could all stand a little more violence."

"Are you suggesting I kill my father?" she whispered. "I'll not—"

"No," Mala cackled. "That would accomplish nothing. You'd become the count, of course, but it would still be expected to join the two houses, and Jera would still be wed to the beastly prince tomorrow evening, and then, pair it with a lovely funeral. And where would you be? Count, sure, but alas, the whole point of becoming count would be useless."

Keneira choked, taking a cloth to her face.

"Though," Mala took another drink. "If something were to happen to the lord and prince tomorrow, I might be inclined to ignore it. Let it be known." Mala winked as she stood from her seat. "I'm not suggesting you do anything. After all, accidents do happen."

CHAPTER 9

K ENEIRA YAWNED AS SHE WALKED her sister up the iron stairs through their home. It was a large home; candles and torches were lit in the lateness of the hour. Looking at her sister, Keneira noted the little girl was rubbing her eyes with her dress. Keneira's mind, as she walked her sister to her bedroom to tuck her in for the night, was infiltrated again by the Count's words; harsh, though they were. Yet, there was a certain subtlety about Count Mala, who presented her with a solution, though not explicitly suggested. Accidents happened, and of course, the killing of Mala's own husband was suggestive enough. Despite the abomination, she doubted she could do go through such a solution. Was there some kind of accident she could concoct that would kill Lorshmo? A pack of hungry dogs perhaps? No, not enough time to make them stave enough for that.

Arriving at the door, she opened it; the iron swung on its hinges, brushed over the dust on the floor before violently berating the wall behind it.

A loud ring echoed through her ears and the eerily empty halls. She led her tuckered sister to her bed, yawning. "I'm not tired," Jera protested, as the door slammed shut behind them, and they were allowed a little peace of mind.

"Come here," Keneira giggled, taking her hand and led her to the bed. "Come, let's get you changed. You've a big day tomorrow. You'll need to be rested."

"I don't like him," Jera growled. "I don't. Why do I have to?"

"Tradition and politics," Keneira sighed. Kneeling down, she brushed a tear from her sister's eye. Her heart felt heavy with sorrow, dread plagued her spirit. One side tried to reconcile these barbaric customs, which no one dared challenge, for they came from the Four Gods. The other side, her will to see her sister all right, was chained forever by the glaring decision, and unwavering will of her father and the king, and that disgusting prince. To marry off a child for their own political gain, even if it meant keeping the lands in relative peace. For better or for worse. What if there was wisdom in that? And the choices of the other counts led to this? Were they to blame?

"But I don't want to; I don't like him, and they will take me from mummy!" she cried. Yes, that was a certainty, for her mother couldn't go with her, not while her corpse lay in a hole in the ground. "Can't you talk to Daddy? Make him change his mind?"

"Hey, hey, hey." She stifled a tear; kept it in so her sister couldn't see the turmoil in her own heart. But there was one thing she thought of that would solve this predicament. She herself could offer herself up as a bride in place of her sister, but then she'd be taken away from Baudet, but she was unwilling to do that, even for her baby sister. "Listen, let's get you to bed. We'll talk more tomorrow."

"But Keneira!" her sister protested, too much. "I don't want to do this!" she cried, kneeling down. Keneira embraced the hug, permitting her sister to cry in her arms. "I don't want to. I don't want to. Let's leave." *And where would we go?*

"I don't know what, or how, but I will do what's good for you," Keneira replied, questioning now what that might be. "Whatever that looks like. Now, Jera, off to bed. You've a busy day tomorrow."

"What will you do?" Her sister changed into a night gown and crawled into bed.

"I don't know," Keneira said. "Hush now, let me think on it." There just wasn't enough time. Tomorrow will be too busy to think.

"Will you hum for me then, to sleep?" Jera asked. "One last time."

"Of course, my dear little princess." *The last time.*

She smiled gravely, and tucked her sister in, stroking her braids. She hummed a tune to her. A made-up tune, for she wasn't musical, but that didn't bother Jera. The little ears complained little when something was out of tune and had not yet completely appreciated the talent others had for music, or perhaps, because this tune came from her own voice, her own beat, made it tolerable. No. That wasn't it at all. It was because it came from Keneira; because, despite its musical flaws, she loved it and thus fell asleep swiftly.

"Sleep well," Keneira whispered, her hand touching her sister's shoulder. Watching her sleep, she didn't dare leave the bed, for she knew not with any level of certainty, if she or her sister would sleep peacefully after tomorrow. This may be the last time she could look at her like this, and so, she would permit herself to abandon her husband in bed tonight. He might not understand, but he would have to accept his lot in life, whatever that lot looked like. Keneira crawled into her sister's bed, and cuddled beside her, arms wrapped around her. The warmth was comforting; like nothing else was in this world. With little hesitation, her eyelids drew themselves closed, and soon, she knew nothing but solace. As much as she could tell, there was little else she could manage, and knew not how long this peace would last.

Chapter 10

D READFULLY, SHE'D NOT THOUGHT OF a lasting solution to her predicament for she couldn't find anything in the halls that she could use to cause a fatal accident. She gazed at her sister, her beautiful, subtle gown, ringlets of gold set upon her hair, pulled back and braided like she had a crown upon her head already. Worthy was her sister, of the grandest of crowns. But not like this, not like the drivel that would be placed on her this evening, not like the drivel of a man, dung heaped, again, balls deep into one of her father's horses! That disgusting little wretch! *My sister!*

A thought entered in her mind. During her own wedding there was a sacrifice of an animal. It was a mere puppy then to account for the wealth Baudet could afford to bring honor and glory to the fabled Four Gods. The priest took the blade and cut the animal open. This time, it was the lord bringing the sacrifice and it was going to be a large boar. She remembered its size and can hear it oinking, too stupid to realize today is its last day alive. The knife must be sharp. *The knife!* But she filed the idea aware that killing Lorshmo with an unsuspecting knife during his wedding might sow chaos. Her family might get caught in the midst of it. She also couldn't imagine herself going through with it.

Jera seemed none too happy either, for why would she be? Not only was the wedding going to take place now, as she was walked into a room with which she would come out and walk down the aisle of the Temple of the Four Gods, but also, her sister had failed, or, Keneira guessed, thought her sister simply did nothing for the sake of tradition. When she became Count, she would do away with all of it, consequences be damned, so no one would have to put up with this Tyranny again.

"I don't want to get mar—"

"You will go through with it," Keneira snapped and relented. "I'm sorry. I'm so sorry. There isn't anything I can do!"

"Fine," her sister sighed, looking down, and then, her eyelids fluttered. Onward then, on a pathway to misery, resigned to her fate.

The door opened, and Keneira took her sister's hand, walking out, crossing the threshold into the temple. The chairs were seated, a fire over yonder toward the altar of the Four Gods. Humanoids, they all were, save for two, of which were fashioned from the dreaded Nezka race, and the Nezkama, the purple bastards. Everyone stood as the music played, and her sister took her first steps, walking as rhythmically as she could, toward the dreadfully dressed king-to-be. The sniveling bastard wiped his nose with his sleeve, sick, no doubt, probably going to die of venereal disease. *You best not touch my sister with your nasty little prick!*

Mala was dressed in a beautiful gown, her ceremonial sword at her hip. A smile on her face as she traded words silently with one of her bodyguards. Not too far from her, closer to the altar of the Four Gods, was Jorgan, dressed in a leather cuirass, but designed for ceremony. He was, after all, expecting trouble, and so was the case with such royal weddings, one could never be too careful. The lord and her father were toward the center, looking at Jera. Keneira refused to scowl as other lesser men ogled her sister.

At last, the moment which she thought would never come, and she let her sister go to join the prince, the two held hands. Keneira no longer could tell the expression her sister had, but she imagined it was none too pleasant. The prince's eyes gleamed with excitement . The man behind him, she knew not his name, but such a man was merely to be the best friend of the groom. No doubt, he would try to turn her husband into a cuckhold, but she'd not have it. No, should the bastard try, he'd have two less fruits.

She stared angrily at the Prince, smiling as he was for a conquest he didn't deserve, was far too distracted to see her glaring at him. The friend, however, seemed to finally avert his gaze from hers, and she looked at him like this throughout the entire ceremony; this angry, foul tradition. She would burn this temple to the ground. For the sake of tradition, and soon. Finally, the sacrifice to cement the marriage. A boar was walked over by the farmer who raised it and brought it to the priest. The priest was about to say the sacrificial rites and raised his hand with a knife, when Keneira interrupted.

"Father, if I may," Keneira said. Was she really considering this? Her gaze shifted to behind the sanctuary, there was a door here, and it led outside. Did she really have it in her? "I'd like to slay it."

"It is strictly forbidden for those of the flock to offer sacrifices to the Four Gods." The priest turned to her, mouth gaped open like she'd gone mad. But she had in fact gone quite insane.

"Yes," she admitted, a sneer crept upon her lips as the prince turned to the king. "It isn't exactly illegal, though, is it? Give me the knife." Seeing the priest didn't comply, she turned to her father. "Father, may I slay the boar?"

"Doesn't matter who slays it." The lord smiled, superseding the request for aid from her father. "Go on, give her the knife. We're to be one house after all."

"Lord Crushma." She grinned as she walked toward the priest, "I thank you."

The priest reluctantly handed her the handle of the knife. Gripping it firmly, she bowed to the priest, a smile creeping on her lips. She was going to do it. Her hand petted the boar, which groaned in reply to her touch, and the knife, ceremonial, handle firm within her grasp, caressed the cheek, the cold iron forced it to jerk away, but her hand reached forth, pulling upon its collar. "There, there, it's going to be all right." With uncertainty, she wasn't sure exactly whose nerves she intended to calm. She took a large breath, the smokey air filled her lungs.

"You bastard!" Keneira cried.

She turned immediately, hearing only a few short gasps at her sudden behavior. With the ceremonial knife, she stabbed Lorshmo in the face, twisting through the bones before pulling it back out. Blood spilled from his wound and he couldn't manage a scream before his lifeless body collapsed. Her eyes shifted again towards the friend, and she grabbed his collar and pulled him close to her sliding the edge of the blade across his neck. Gargling, he collapsed down the small set of stairs leading towards the rest of the pews, and with her bloody one, she took her sister's hand. "We're getting out of here"

Her sister squealed at the blood. Some sprayed upon her face as she stumbled and jerked away. The priest didn't have enough time to respond; no one did, save for the screaming and confusion of creaking chairs scratching across the floor. The boar still growled, for it lived to see another day, or perhaps after tonight, someone would enjoy a bountiful meal. Disappearing behind the altar, Keneira knew she'd be hunted. She needed her sword! Any sword; didn't have to be hers. Unfortunately, her husband was caught in the middle of the madness. Now, he would remain a stableboy, and it would be like her marriage never happened because the hammer of the false justice of a lord will fall upon her house. But it was just a ceremony. Her love for him wasn't dependent upon it. She had only hoped he had sense enough to leave the temple before it was too late.

***

"Lorshmo! My Son!" Crushma cried, running over to his son's fallen corpse. "Get her! Kill her!"

Of course he was detestable, but he was still Crushma's son.

He pulled his son from the ground, nearly unrecognizable, wiping the blood from his son's face. His beloved child, his only one, lay dead with a slit into his face, bones cracked underneath that dreadful woman's knife. Kira, he would pay for this. *He would hang!* Gritting his teeth, he looked at the count, who, undoubtedly, wanted this. He put Keneira up to this! "Bring me his head!"

"Sire," Kira spoke gently. "It grieves me, truly, it does. But I did not tell her to do this."

"And yet you respond as if knowing my thoughts," Crushma snapped.

"They are impossible not to know, my lord," Kira replied. "Jorgan, go fetch them. Bring Jera back to us alive. If it is impossible, then kill Keneira. She is no daughter of mine."

"Don't you dare, he'll help her escape!" Crushma protested. "Mala!"

He looked at the only other count who could be bothered to show up to this wedding. "Seize him!"

"That won't be necessary," Jorgan replied, hand on his pommel.

"Necessary!" Crushma swore. "Curse this house. Curse all of it. We all know you mentored the girl in sword play. You can't be trusted."

"My loyalty has never been in question," Jorgan replied. "Trust me when I say it belongs to this house, and this house alone. Kira has already declared that Keneira does not belong to this house anymore. I will kill her and bring back Jera."

"But you cannot bring back my son!" Crushma wept. "Go. Someone hang Kira!"

"And then the house will die!" Jorgan said. "He is the Count!"

"I don't think that's necessary," Mala spoke up. Crushma watched her whispering something with one of her messengers. "I think we can hold off on any executions for the treasonous bitch. But the Nezkama are coming. They appear to have broken off from the rest and are making their way here. Seems they really wanted a bloody wedding," she laughed. "Well, they got one!"

"Fine," Crushma agreed.

There was a ruckus in the crowd, still too shocked to move to permit them to process anything other than the two bodies on the floor, murdered in cold blood. But there was one person who was moving outside his own agency. A man trying to escape. The king gestured immediately. "Seize that man!" Men and women clad in armor grabbed him, he stopped struggling, and was escorted to the king. The king recognized the stableboy; this was the man with whom Keneira shared the cup.

"Where will your wife go?" Crushma asked. He turned to the messenger. "See to it word gets out: a king's gold reward will go to the man who brings me her head."

"Milord," Mala snapped. "You clearly are out of touch with the count's subjects. They don't want money; it's useless. All that will do is provide reason for others to come and steal from them. Offer them a seat at your table for food; indefinitely."

"No," he said. "Another mouth to feed—"

"Well, you've a prince no more, so I think you can afford it," Mala suggested.

Crushma gritted his teeth; Count Mala wasn't replaceable, and she knew it. A bastard of a combination to have amongst the ranks, someone worth more than their weight in gold and untold riches, and likely, knew it. Drit circumstances, but he would deal with it later. He always did. But now, to this man. "Answer me!"

Grieved as everyone was, soldiers from the ranks started to depart by way of orders from their captains, to prepare the way for despair, and the violence which would ensue shortly. Why, why couldn't he get a minute to grieve? *Damn Nezkama bastards!*

"No!" Baudet said; that was his name, Crushma remembered. "No."

"Every man has his price," Mala said, tilting Keneira's husband's face to her, a gleam in her eye. "What's yours?"

***

"No," Baudet replied.

Mala observed Jorgan depart from the temple, and shook her head as she grabbed rope and tied the stableboy's hands together, and pointed to the other count. "Funrik, tie up Kira, will you? We'll hang them before we take everything outside. You and I need to prepare for a siege."

Kira begged as he was bound in ropes, and the stable boy seemed quite composed of himself as he was dragged by a small procession of soldiers, of whom, Mala had command as the King was left to mourn his son's early departure from the Land of Dreams. Funrik grunted as nooses were made, and they dragged the two guilty parties and were fastened tightly to the nooses before they were pulled up, and they just hanged, struggling to their last breath. Sighing heavily, maintaining her act, she glanced over to Funrik, who stared gravely at the horizon. No longer able to ignore it, heaps of fiery metal soared through the air, crashing into houses. The citizenry of this fief was in disarray as they screamed for help.

"What are your orders, Mala?" The swordmaster bowed. "My sword is yours to command for the time being."

"Yes." Mala walked over to him, and pressed against his shoulders. "There's only one thing you need to do."

She wrapped her arm around his neck, and pulled him top her, impaling him with her ceremonial sword. He struggled, but she twisted the blade as he collapsed to the ground, and with a swing, sliced his throat. She wiped the blade clean from the murder. She couldn't risk the sword master getting in the way of her own plans. That would make an already messy wedding even more chaotic.

CHAPTER 11

KENEIRA FLED WITH HER SISTER toward the armory that was farther down the hallway. She didn't have time to get her own sword, so a practice blade would have to do. Running, panting, sweating, her little sister too, hands on her thighs as she bent over, breathing heavily. Thanks to the Four Gods, they don't dress up as fabulously for weddings as the dastardly women in the South. Finally, they reached the armory, and she found a sword, tied it to her waist, and just in case, scoured over the weaponry with the smith and foundries unattended. She found a crossbow and some bolts, a good, solid, one-hundred-fifty pounds worth.

She took her sister's clammy hands in her own. "We're getting you out of here." *South? Yes, we'll be safe there.* "Look," she said. "I know it's hard, but we have to keep running. We'll go places they cannot or will not follow."

"But we're leaving mummy," Jera whined. Of course, she'd be sad about it, the one such course of

Keneira's actions. What other consequences await her tonight? After all, she did not once think this through. "Mummy!"

"Jera," Keneira put her hand on her sister's shoulders. "You were going to be separated regardless; I wish things could be different. I'm saving you." *Was she?* Or was this something she was trying to convince herself of? "I have a friend down in the slums. We can stay with him, take a moment, and think before they come looking for us."

Exactly how much time had passed? It certainly hadn't been a full day, and yet, a spirit of sleep was coming upon her. She knew she had to stay awake, for she knew not what she was going to do, or for how much longer she'd have to force herself awake.

"Very well," her sister wiped her tears, and hugged her "Thank you, for saving me."

"Thank me not yet," Keneira replied. *What else am I going to lose tonight?* By the Four Gods, she wished she had thought this through.

Dreadfully aware of the uproar throughout the fief, people scampering about, wheels carting as if there was nothing to see. Horses roamed, pulling the carts along. Some people rested, stayed inside their own little homes of iron walls, and some candles lit here, some torches there. She needed a light herself; where to find one? No telling really, when she might need to traverse the Abyss, which was almost an inevitable fate, for there was not enough light in the night to traverse the roads. Was she mad?

When they arrived at the door of Mirkur, her sister tugged on her hand firmly. Keneira sighed, squatting with her free hand touching the door. "Jera, it's all right. I know you don't know him, but he's a good person. We can trust him, if no one else." Jera nodded, grunting with the pain in her thigh. Keneira had noticed it during their sprint to the armory. They had no choice really. Keneira nodded, showing her sister she understood her pain, then stood up and knocked on the iron door.

Footsteps echoed from behind it and a light illuminated from the crack underneath the door. At last, it pulled open, and a man with a slender face, a weak smile, and above all, rags that smelled of flies stood in the doorway. Father, another companion of whom he simply would not approve. His smile brightened upon seeing who it was, and with nervousness, his eye seemed to be looking at something past her.

"Keneira," he said. "Lovely to see you again; it's been ages. Since you've been married, I think."

"Aye, Mirkur. I agree, it's been too long," she said. "May we come in? This is my sister."

"Of course," he spoke sharply. "Hurry."

Keneira walked in with her sister, permitting Mirkur to shut the door quietly so as not to arouse suspicion from any suspecting pursuers. She led her sister to the table, and hoisted her up to a stool so she could sit in relative comfort. She took an intense inhalation and permitted herself a moment to think as Mirkur walked over, sitting across.

"What's your name?" he asked.

"It's—it's—" Jera began to say.

"It's all right," Keneira leaned in close to her sister, their cheeks kissing. "It's all right, you can tell him."

"J-Jera," she stammered.

"Lovely name." Mirkur smiled. "I trust, based on the attire, that you came from a wedding. Yours?"

"A—aye—" she replied.

"Look," Keneira spoke. "We need your help."

"Well, by the looks of it, you murdered the groom." Mirkur pointed to the blood on Jera's face. "Now, I may not be a smart man, but I recognize blood when I see it. Please, tell me who it was?"

"You don't know?"

"Four Gods," he said, with gaping eyes. "The prince. You didn't kill the prince. Tell me, Keneira! Did you, or did you not kill the prince?"

She heard scattering footsteps from above the ceiling. "Yes," she admitted. "A foul man, if ever there was one."

"We're all foul," he said, with a fading smile. "You need to leave. I thought you'd be in trouble, but I didn't think this. Your being here puts my family at risk. I'd do many things for you, Keneira, but not this. Leave immediately! I'll speak of your presence to no one. Get out. The back door you can use, now leave before—"

"Keneira!" a voice called from the other side. *Drit.* "We've come for Keneira, come out now. We know she's in there!"

Mirkur stood from the table, walked briskly to the counter, palms slapping the surface. He pulled out a drawer and grabbed a kitchen knife. Turning to her, the knife behind his back, he opened his mouth. "Out the back! Now. You brought them here!" Terror seized his face. "You must leave!" He turned to go to the door as she helped her sister from the stool. Fear gripped her, and she bit her lip until red blood dripped out from her mouth.

"Come," she said, quietly walking toward the back of the house.

"She's not here," Mirkur said. "Get yer own food. I've not enough to spare. You know that."

"I don't want yer food; now, open the damned door, peasant bastard!"

"That's just ru—"

The door swung open, knocking him in the face. Mirkur dropped to the ground, the knife behind his back flew out and spun on the floor. Keneira looked away as she hurried to the window, footsteps echoing behind her. "Keneira! Get over here. Get back here!" She hoisted her sister out the window of the house, and her little body scurried like a rat, looking for cover.

"Hide!" She felt a hand on her shoulder. Before she could vault herself out the window, she was pulled and thrown onto the ground, landing painfully on her back. "Gah!" she grunted; the man jumped atop her. Before she could grab her sword, his hands were around her throat, squeezing tightly. Gritting her teeth, unable to breathe, she pushed her fingers into the man's throat, but he was too stubborn.

Mirkur lifted the man up, the knife in his hand, and thrust it into his chest. The man grunted as Mirkur twisted the blade then pulled it out as blood poured to the ground. Another wound, another pierce, and he pulled out again, until the crimson liquid painted the floor and the soldier fell to the ground. Mirkur took a bloody hand and helped Keneira up from the ground, as another cry, one she didn't know, sounded. "It's her! She's here!"

"Get out!" Mirkur cried. "Now!"

He pushed her; she tripped on the window ledge and landed on a bed of hay, flies buzzing around her. The smell of shit permeated the air, and her heart pounded along with the screams coming from inside the house. She stood and looked back briefly; Mirkur was a bloody mess, barely recognizable. She remembered the old man from years ago, and he was always kind to her. Some of the kindest people didn't have much. But her heart sank briefly as she knew he was dead and to see him in such a state filled her with such dread. The grief only lasted so long as she was reminded that the men inside were looking for her, shrieking like one bloody K'hara. The bird of the air of the Abyss; a foul thing. She turned, saw her sister whimpering behind an iron box, and she took her hand, and pulled her up immediately.

"Run, Jera, run!" she ordered.

Keneira's heart felt like it was going to burst through her chest. Her feet took her without orders to the main pathway, and she heard the cries of those calling for her head coming from behind. She turned her head again, the blood and markings of Mirkur flashed through her, and sweat beaded through her palms, so she squeezed her sister's hand tighter. Her legs lifted with longer strides, as several people came running at her with violent dogs and pitch forks.

She turned her gaze forward, and people poured out onto the streets as if someone relayed information of her treason. Word could get out quickly here, for reasons she knew not, but she kept running. A loud cackle here, whistling wind there, pushing through the cracks between the houses and brushing past her hair. She nearly fell over, and into scattering debris, fecal matter, hay, and bits and pieces of stone.

"Give us the girl! Give her to us!" someone called, hurling a pitchfork at her. She pivoted her feet and the fork thrust right past her head, scratching her face. Hissing, she gritted her teeth and gripped her sister firmly, ignoring her screams of terror. Her heart pumped, beating in her ears.

"You won't take her!" she swiveled back, as the crowd of people advanced. Bolting away as fast as she could, getting closer to the road, which of course, put her in the path of the Abyss; the one place she wouldn't be followed. "Stay away from my sister!"

A loud crash sounded behind her. The buildings creaked as they struck against the flesh of her pursuers. The people inside screamed in agony as their own flesh, bones, and blood littered the earth behind her. Only one thing made in this land could collapse buildings. Catapults. Were they that desperate to come after her? Wait. No. This was far worse. Smoldering flames scoured over the land, of all things that could be burned. A loud horn, three blasts it made. Three for war. She didn't have time to remember if it was the Nezka, or the Nezkama that the lord managed to piss off recently, but the timing couldn't possibly be any worse!

Horses galloped, clopping their hooves against the stone coming from the right side of her. Hissing and swearing, she was certain had she not gone to the privy before rescuing her sister; she should have shat her pants ages ago. Her ears rang as she neared the stones leading out of the village, heading farther away from the village, and closer still, toward the Abyss. The soldiers on the horses were clad with armor and lances as they came forward. Snarls and glares to her left side, she saw giant wolves and goats ripping up the terrain with their strides, and the Nezka... *that's who he pissed off...* rode upon them, wielding flails and scythes.

"Keep running!" she cried, as if to assure herself her little sister would run.

Strides came forth with the shaking of the ground. Cries of battle pierced her ears as the hordes came, encroaching upon them. Wolves howled, horses neighed, iron creaked, and metal clashed. Shrieks of pains and whines of wolves followed, and the dying screeches of horses after that. Chest pounding, Keneira panted, sweat dripping from her face. She refused to be separated from Jera, who screeched in terror, a high-pitched wail. At times, she couldn't tell what it was; the sound of battle around her was too fierce and far too loud.

"Keneira!" a loud cry, from a warrior on horseback. She didn't recognize the voice. Rearing his horse, he charged at her. She breathed quickly, looking to the ground as the rider hunted her, and a loose cobblestone was what she found. Reaching out, the moving of horses distracted her for a moment. Lifting up the stone, she hurled it at the horse. Its leg buckled, and it neighed loudly as the armored rider was flipped off at her feet. His neck cracked, but at least he was alive. She quickly pulled out her sword, stabbed him in the neck, and sheathed it, before she could let the guilt weigh in upon her soul.

Keneira continued to run; the soldiers were too distracted with one another, and with what she thought amounted to several turns of the hour glass, she finally made it out of the fray, blood soaking her clothes. Suddenly, a Nezka came at her, a large creature with a war hammer. Grimacing, she pushed her sister to the side as the beast struck at her. Jumping to the opposite flank, the strike hit the ground. Drawing her sword, she struck at the Nezkama's hands, slicing off his fingers. Then, with a deft flick of her wrist, she impaled him in the chest, twisting the blade before ripping it out. All before the purple bastard could scream.

Behind the fallen corpse of the Nezkama, she beheld the ruins they left behind. Men, women, and Nezkama, all lay on the ground with numerous wounds to their body, many trampled from the strides and struggles of various beasts. Both horses and wolves littered the ground, and a few pockets of foot soldiers survived, fighting with no hesitancy, and with neither side willing to give an inch.

"Come!"

"I'm scared!" her sister wailed. "And you- you're hurting me!"

Keneira shook her head and released her grip. "I'm sorry, but we have to go."

"But Keneira!" her sister cried, tears streaming down her face. "My legs."

"Then I'll carry you!" Keneira said without hesitation, put her hands between her sister's armpits, hoisted her up, and started walking away from the scene of battle. "But remember, when we get to the Abyss, I must stop to light a lantern."

"Very well," Jera conceded, as she embraced her.

Chapter 12

KENEIRA AND JERA ARRIVED AT the road, the flames still lit around from the chaos of missed shot catapults. Oil burned; the scent was rancid. Crinkling her nose, Keneira looked around her. Surprisingly, there was no sound, save for the distant clashing sound of battle. A siege like this only ended one way, and that was only the survival of those who knew where the food was. The humans of the north would slay the Nezka and enslave them; they always did. And then, they'd regroup their efforts to find her. If the lord was persuasive enough, they'd even dare traverse the Abyss.

"All right," she said, letting her sister down. She opened the lantern from its top, pulled out some tinder, and lit it. "You're on foot now; remember, stay close to me. And if we're ever separated, don't go into the darkness."

"What if there's nowhere else to go?" she asked, one hand tightened into a fist. She bit it gently.

That was a reality far too likely for her liking. There was little that could be assured in a time like this, with opportunities running amuck for anyone looking for whatever it was the lord promised them for her head. Keneira clicked her tongue as she looked her sister in the eyes, attempting to give her an assuring smile as her soul searched for the right words. There was nothing significant that came to mind, and while the truth was far from reassuring, she chose to tell her. "Then do whatever seems best to you. But don't wander too far into the dark that you can't find the light again. Whenever you do, look up, and look for the green orbs in the sky."

"They're gone." Her sister pointed.

"For now, yes," Keneira said. "But there are lanterns scattered across the road. And when the morning comes, the green lights will guide you back to safety on the road. Do you trust me?"

"Yes," her sister said. "More than anyone else."

Keneira hoped her sister hadn't misplaced her trust.

They walked along the road. The pathway was still lit by the torch set apart to provide the first sanctuary from the Abyss. The light from her lantern pushed the darkness away as she approached. The black fog tried to penetrate the light, but to no avail, thank the Four Gods! She forced herself and her sister along with hastened steps, and it was not too long before they were completely surrounded by the Abyss, the preliminary torch no longer in sight; neither was the next torch in the road, not yet.

Her heart raced, then settled. Just silence, minus the creaking of her lantern which swayed on one side of her and their steps, making their way across the road, and the occasional screech from an animal. A familiar one she'd heard before, but thankfully, didn't see what made it. The K'hara, probably; great birds that flew above the Abyss at all hours. They were more active when the green lights faded. Luckily, they were one horror that would stay away from the light at all costs. She and her sister arrived at another milestone, where a stone held an iron rod impaled, and upon it, a lantern. An orb of light, one in which would give them a sense of ease as the arms of the Abyss tried to penetrate this barrier, and again, to no success. For now, they were safe.

Or so she thought.

Armor clanked in the distance from the direction they had come. Clopping hooves and a flame. Jorgan came at her, riding on a horse with a lance. A light on the horse's side. A scowl upon his face. The horse neighed violently as he pushed the beast toward the light. The darkness tried to claim him, but the light was too strong, even from that measly lantern. Blood was caked against his face, and one of his arms hung limply at his side. The horse reared into the light and his lance was aimed at her.

Her mentor, her protector. That's the role he was to play; his tradition. She gritted her teeth as if someone stabbed her heart, trying to rip it from her chest. He trained her for years in swordplay, taught her the value of tradition, despite how religiously she tried to escape it, but now, here he was abandoning his tradition. No. That wasn't it. His tradition was, and always would be, tied to the House, and through Keneira's actions tonight, the House had all but fallen. Killing her wasn't betrayal. By killing her, he would be fulfilling his tradition.

"Stay in the light!" she cried, pulling her sister away, releasing her grip. *Don't stray too far.*

She knew in her heart Jorgan would seek to fulfil his duty, and considering the individual context she found herself in, with blood on her hands that likely meant he was commissioned by the lord to seek her head. And to deliver Jera back to them. She didn't want to think what the lord would do to her sister.. Her heart sank as she feared for her own life. As she feared for her sister, but as her thoughts spiraled out of control she realized something. Killing Lorshmo was one thing. Killing a *swordmaster* was different, especially now since she had a personal relationship to this one. If she could, could she go through with killing Jorgan? She only hoped that she could put an end to this madness, or talk him out of his tradition.

Jorgan got closer, too, with the spearhead meant to impale her. Drawing her sword, she swept it up, striking the lance. The horse ran past her as the tip of the spear flew up, the metal clanking at the strike. The horse ran into the abyss, but the light protected him. Rearing the horse around, he threw, and the spear soared at her. She leaned backwards, dodging. He drew his sword and charged at her. The horse's hooves drowned out her sister's screams. Her sword, clutched with two hands, aimed for the horse. Nearing her, Jorgan's blade slashed. She ducked. The blade barely missed her. She cried out, twisting her body as she struck the horse's hind legs with all her strength.

The horse neighed, tumbling down. Jorgan was thrust off the back of the horse, rolling off to the side. He stared at her, getting up before she could attempt to strike at him again. His gaze, stern as it was, looked at her with rage before turning to his steed. His blade in hand, he walked over to the beast, on its side now, and he impaled its head.

"Give Jera over to me, Keneira, and I might let you live," he said, baring his teeth at her; a dark mood must have plagued his spirit. "Stop running."

"No." She shook her head. "You can't have her!"

The emotions inside her heart raged, but it was also filled with despair. *Jorgan. No.* Her thoughts were filled and muddied with conflict. She didn't want to be pitted against her mentor. She didn't want to leave Jera to the horrible fate that no doubt awaited her should he take her back to the lord. She didn't want to kill Jorgan, but her fear was soon to be realized that she may very well have to do that to save her sister. Her mind steadied, with her free hand at her hip, nursing a small strain.

"Then I'll kill you!" He lunged forward but stopped when his leg gave out.

"You'd have not offered me the chance if you thought you could take me," she said, realizing he is also conflicted. "Least of all." She pointed her sword toward him. "Not in your current condition."

"Had you the stance you had yesterday, it matters little." He frowned at her, his sword raised in response. "We're here because of your actions, Keneira. You are the best student I've ever had. This makes it all the more difficult. Don't make me kill you!"

"You can let me go," Keneira said, brows furrowed. *Don't make me kill you.* "You can live. Just abandon your tradition, and then it's over, and we can leave."

The night was short, and the road, long. She wanted it to be over, but the longer she tarried here, the more time people would have to organize and hunt her, should the battles be over. She hoped earnestly that there was something inside her teacher that would permit him to throw caution to the wind, but actions had consequences. In an ideal world, she never would have asked this of herself, nor asked him to abandon the values he held above everything else. But this world was far from ideal, and no amount of cruelty within the grim pits of despair and violence and starvation would change that.

"You don't get to decide when it's over," he said, there was no tremble in his voice. "You don't get to uproot tradition. You don't get to change the will of the lord!" Sharp were his words before he released a sigh from his lips. "I gave you an out; just walk through the Abyss, leave your sister to me, and it will be over. Just leave!"

"You know I can't do that." Now she felt herself frowning; the weight of emotional distance between them darkening. As bleak as the Abyss is at night. As bleak as a world without fire.

"Then this will be the last fight one of us will know."

"So be it."

Keneira clashed with him. Sword against sword, her shoes and his boots in the mud and blood of the horse, spraying, slipping. His strong strikes were significantly weaker than she was used to; clearly, he had been wounded by a Nezka. However, he was still admirable, pivoting against strikes he normally would have taken. A slash struck toward her, but she parried it with the pommel, twisting her body and pushing him aside. His free hand twisted into a fist, punching her square in the face. *The dirty trick!*

He swung his blade. She bent backwards, but the steel nearly nicked her nose, and she stepped farther from him. Dancing, she returned to her feet again, her stance as firm as she could manage. He thrust his sword at her again, and she twisted herself to permit the thrust to pass her. She struck his wrist with her pommel, *hard*. The blade came free. She swiveled her blade to his throat, but he pivoted before she could kill him and parried the strike. His blade clamored into the Abyss, and he charged at her, tackling her to the ground.

"Keneira!" her sister cried. "Jorgan, stop this, please!"

"No!" was his response. "These are the damned consequences!"

Keneira felt a strike to her face, the back of her head hitting the ground. Grunting, her hand stretched to his waist and pulled out the dagger he kept tucked away. She impaled him under his armor and twisted the blade. He grunted, grimacing. She pushed him off and rolled atop him, ripping the blade out as she did. She looked him in the eye, a man well respected for his prowess in battle; terror was written upon his face as he was bested. The knife impaled his neck, his screams silent in the light.

Keneira's mentor was dead. She leaned back and dropped the blade. Blood pooled, and already, she started to feel it wet her buttocks as she sat in the mess. Her hands shook. She stared down, and felt a presence behind her. Her hands weighed with guilt. Lorshmo was dead. She didn't regret it, but perhaps the consequences were put into her hands. The nameless soldier and Nezka whom she killed. Self-defense. But her mentor, here as he lay, was silent. This was a life taken she felt she would carry to the end of her days.

"Keneira." Her sister's high-pitched voice brought her back to the present. Her right hand immediately grabbed hold of her sister's arm. *All for you. I did all this for you.* Her teeth ground, she took the knife, and hurled it into the Abyss, screaming. Just a little peace, that's all she wanted. But now, there is only one choice. Ignoring her sister's pleas for attention, she stood.

"Ha," she grunted. A sharp pain hit through her abdomen. Limping, she reached for her sword, and put it to her waist, strapping Jorgan's to her other side. "Come, Jera, we must get going." She turned, grabbed hold of the lantern, and looked toward the South, away from the fief she knew.

Keneira took her free hand and pulled her sister to her side. Someone was bound to hear the screams of their battle; there was no time to waste contemplating her actions. Oh, lords, why did she not think this through?

"Very well," Jera spoke, her hair tucked behind her ears. She would make someone happy, but not that bastard prince.

"We keep walking, until we're far away from this place, and we can rest," she said. "Then, we'll see the whole world!"

What kind of promise was that? This world was dark, plant life barely existed, and that tree, that fruit from yesterday, was the liveliest thing she'd come across in ages. There was food there, and water.

Assuming they even could get there, it was a safe place to go and hide as she knew no one else knew about it. But getting there would be no small feat, and she didn't want to risk it unless absolutely necessary with the battle raging. The flowers died, the vegetables died, and those that were deemed unfit for human consumption were tossed to the animals, or eaten among the living.

Breathing heavily, in pain, her gaze looked downward. Her eyes gaped open in terror, and she looked back up. The Abyss still remained undisturbed, save for a few lights, traversing it with lanterns. Scores of footsteps, marching toward her, from the one direction she intended to go. Her way had been cut off. She could traverse the Abyss, but the pain she was in, she doubted she could outrun a beast, or the corruption inside it, or the K'hara especially, still screeching.

What if she were to kill Lord Crushma? Tradition would come crumbling down with him. There would be no central power, and the counts would struggle, fighting one another for the next several years for the lord's crown. During war with the Nezka, perhaps assassination might not be the best course of action, then the humans of the west would end up enslaved to the Nezka. But she was also uncertain if it was Nezka troops in front of her, or the lord's men. She let out a sigh; there was no good option here. Just the best bad one. But she must keep her sister close. Or else all her efforts would be meaningless.

"Hey," she said, kneeling down. "We're going to go back."

"Why?" her sister whined. "I don't want to go back to those awful men."

"Our way is blocked," she said, pointing to the Abyss with the faint orange hue of moving flames. "See there? We cannot survive the Abyss for long, so we must go back. I will not let him have you. You hear me, Jera? I will not let anyone take you."

"I understand," Jera said.

Keneira took her hand and turned. As they passed Jorgan's body, her sister said, "I really liked him."

"I—I know," Keneira stammered. "I did, too. There's not much we can do now, though, just head forward."

CHAPTER 13

THE FIEF WAS OVERTURNED. FLAMES still soared, and volunteers were pulling the dead off the streets, dragging them into larger pits, before setting them aflame. Corpses of animals were cut up into manageable chunks, discarded into wheelbarrows, and blood coated the land. There would be no time to recover, and the fighting had all but ceased, but the sound of the marching band behind them meant it was still on its way, and in Keneira and Jera's escape path. Keneira had to find a place to hide her. A place that wouldn't be searched again. A place away from the mess of battle, and bloodlust.

Her sister whimpered again. Animals were dying, things she loved, and things Keneira took for granted. What was the point of any of it? No. She mustn't think like that, not for her sister. She turned to her, knelt down, and clasped her hands over Jera's. "I need you to be quiet," she whispered. "We're going farther in, and we can put an end to their hunt. I will come back to kill that bastard lord," her teeth ground, "and maybe we can save our house and not have to leave. Unless we do that, they will never stop hunting us. I need to get closer, but…"

"You'll die," her sister said. "Everyone will."

"Not today," Keneira assured her sister. She knelt down, held her sister's shoulders within her palms tightly. "If I can kill Jorgan, I can kill the lord. I need you to stay close, though; I can't have you getting too far from me. Stop whimpering, stop grieving, there will be time for it, just not now. You hear me, Jera?"

"Very well," Jera said, and put her free hand over her mouth.

"Good girl," Keneira whispered.

She led her sister through the fief. Well, what was left of it. Shattered remains of buildings, weapons and shields broken, wrenched into pieces of steel and iron. Even the arrows were bent out of shape. Moving farther, she heard a distant scream, another battle horn, and the soldiers of the north went back to war. The Nezka prepared another offensive, another rush, and fortunately, most had completely forgotten there was a prize for her head. Amazing what one forgets when war is at the front door.

They crept through the fief, along a steady line of steel bars and rope. Keneira heard creaking, and looking upwards, she saw several bodies swaying in the wind. Blood covered their faces, but she recognized them. Her body turned, and she held her sister close so Jera wouldn't see her father hanging there.

There were no two ways about it: this was her doing, and her fault, just to save her sister. *Was it worth it?*

"Cover your eyes," she said. "I don't want you to see this."

"See what?" Jera asked.

"Trust me," Keneira assured her. "You. Do. Not. Want. To see this."

She fought with everything she had not to choke up. Not to make a sound that would startle her sister as she watched her own father hang in the air. Lifeless. Eyes bulging. Hands limped at his side as his body simply stayed there. Her heart sank when she found him. First her mother. Now her father. He was a cruel and barbaric man whom she found few redeeming qualities within him. The principal evidence being the events that led to this marriage. As much as she had grown to detest him, he was still her father.

But worse so when she realized who hanged beside him. Her husband Baudet was in the same condition and she hoped that the fall killed him, rather than the hanging. But she looked closely at him. Blood marks were at his neck, as if he tried clawing his way free but with no avail. Her heart broke repeatedly these last few days, but she needed to be strong for Keneira, and realized she needed to take her own advice. Grieve later. Now simply wasn't the time for such luxuries.

Baudet. She realized much too late she should have told him not to go to the wedding.

She watched as her sister closed her eyes. Leaning forward, she pulled her sister close to her, and her chest puffed with tears. Shrugging, she came to the realization that unless she replaced the king, her house had indeed fallen to decay. The king lay claim to it, for however long he chose to keep it. Her heart was breaking inside, but she mustn't concern Jera with it. This was her problem to fix.

She hoisted her sister and walked her up the path toward the temple, but off the path so they wouldn't be seen. Refreshed as the Nezkama might be, the northern humans were tough. They knew pain, and knew how to suffer, a virtue of which the dirty little devils simply knew not. She found a small barn and she put her sister inside, hidden within the creaking walls.

"Stay here," she said. Her sister need not follow her. It would be needlessly distracting.

"Don't leave!" her sister pleaded, clutching tightly to her forearm. "I don't want to be alone."

"You won't be alone." Keneira pointed at the chickens. "I'll be back. Like I said, Jera, I will not let them have you." She had lost too much already. She wouldn't lose her sister, too. "Remember, be quiet; don't let anyone see you until I come get you."

"But what if you don't come back?" her sister pleaded. She'd seen death enough to know of the possibility.

"I will come back. I won't die, you'll see. Just stay here," Keneira replied, turning before she could see the tears in her sister's eyes.

I killed a sword master. I can kill a lord.

***

The count marveled at the field of corpses. Her own blade was not kept clean, nor her body unbattered. Stepping over mounds and mounds of bodies, blood flowed through the streets of this once profitable fief. Some of the bodies moved, others remained dead. Peering over the side of the streets, buildings were leveled to the ground. Limbs of human, and Nezka alike were scattered from their bodies, strewn on the ground, and other torsos had been trampled by horses. Men. Women. Children. Innocent. Guilty. No one, and nothing were separated from the carnage, especially the small house cats.

Startled, she kicked her boot away when a woman cried out to her.

"Milady," she said. "Help."

Mala raised her boot high, before stomping on the peasant's skull, her brains oozing onto the stone. "Prepare for a feast!" Mala ordered. "Get all this meat on wagons and cover them with salt. The rest, prepare for a meal."

"But our friends—" a soldier nearby cried out.

"Your friends are dead." She pointed a firm finger at him. "They're food now. We can't let them go to waste."

"Count Mala!" a soldier cried, running over the bodies, tripping. "I found Jera."

"Keneira? Jorgan?"

"Jorgan was found dead," he panted. "Keneira is nowhere to be found."

"She's likely going for the head of the lord," she sneered. However, she knew in the eyes of the rest of the counts, the marriage would have still been considered consummated, despite its circumstances. Just a fabricated truth. Crushma was known for that in his years of leadership. "Take me to Jera. We must keep her safe."

"Of course," he said, and he took her to a barn just a mile from the funeral pyre where the lord's son was still likely burning. The girl huddled up against a post, and a dog barked at her. Mala knelt down and offered a hand.

"This is no place for a little girl," she said. "Come with me."

"But—"

"You'd like to see Keneira," Mala said. "Wouldn't you?"

"No!" the brat smacked her hand away.

"Your sister was right, you know," Mala reasoned. "Your marriage to that brat should never have been on the table. I'm on your side in all this, really, I am."

"You mean that?"

"Of course." Mala smiled, taking the hand of the now compliant girl. "Come, let's go find your sister."

Chapter 14

THE TEMPLE OF THE FOUR Gods was close. They reigned supreme, with their superfluous ideals, imposed upon people who would never know them personally. Mournful music played by her father's musicians; the king obviously spared them, but not others of the house. Of *her* house. That was the price of her actions. She crept up and beheld the king in the center of the circle by the bonfire. On it lay his son, on fire, cremating. The ashes of his corpse rising to the Abyss above them.

Keneira's hand rested on the pommel of her sword. She'd kill the lord, right here in front of all these people. If her house were to die tonight, so too would the Westlands. What kind of lord would force her sister to marry his bastard son, just to legitimize his debauchery? What was she supposed to do now? There were no good options for her to choose from. Was it too late? No. She'd never turn her back on Jera. Well, best do it now and get it over with.

"Crushma!" She darted from the shadows, charging at the king.

He turned, grieving lines upon his face, and a lone hand rested on his pommel. Armed to the teeth, and armored heavily with chain mail, and leather patches, he twisted his stance to face her. Eyes red with tears and swollen. His sad face turned irate, and he grimaced as he pulled his sword and parried hers with ease, kicked her, and slashed at her. She parried the strike, but realized the strike he made was merely a defensive stroke and nothing else.

"Keneira," he spoke solemnly; she swung back at him. Pivoting his feet, a swift tilt to his back ensured he'd not get wounded. "You kill a man's son, and as he's grieving, and you seek to take his life. Why would you do this?"

"You know very well why." She gritted her teeth. "I walked past my husband and father hanging! That only proves my resolve was correct." Who was she trying to convince, exactly? "You tried to marry my sister into your family."

"It was your father's choice!" he snapped, wincing eyes and tears escaped, dripping down his cheek. She gasped. Could it be true? "I sent word to all the counts with eligible daughters, and he made his choice. Yes, yes, my son has unique tastes, I know that, but I'd never force a count to decide. They had options."

"I don't believe you," Keneira said.

All this time had passed, had her father misled her? Were there options on the table, but only this one was apparent? Or could it be because of Lorshmo's appetites that options were few. No, if even her father declined, there would have been a forced ceremony anyway. But then she realized something. A forced ceremony would have been preferable now, as it would have been with someone else, and her family wouldn't have been thrust into this barbaric choice, and in her heart, she knew now more so than ever. One should never presume to make a choice, for choices themselves are an evil.

"Then trust me when I say, your father was the only one willing to submit his daughter to this, to submit your sister!" He pointed. "Who's the real devil here? My son? The filthy swine? I can't help that. Me, for providing him with options? You, who killed my son? Or your father, who offered Jera so willingly? It seems that our fates are more intertwined than you think."

"No, they're not," she snapped. "They're *not*. I'll kill you for what you did to my House!"

"What *I* did?" He scoffed. "You're a *child*! If you had not killed my son, they would still be alive. You'd still be heir to the count's seat. Your treasonous attempt to subvert your father's decision led to that, not me. Your house and mine were tied. Success and failure depended on the other. If the marriage had happened, that union would make things more stable, and the line of kings would continue. Now, there is no line, and when I die, we'll be thrust into chaos! Is that what you wanted?"

"Of course not," Keneira replied. "I just want to kill you."

"Stupid girl!"

Keneira grimaced and charged at him. Their swords clashed and the metal clanged. Keneira moved forward steadily; after all, Jorgan trained her, but he was not the best teacher in the land. The best was always reserved for the king. She pivoted, tired, but her legs proved to be true, and the lord, older in years, was still nimble, dancing back and forth, pulling his blade to try to feint her. They nicked each other's sides multiple times but drew no substantial blood. Grimacing, Keneira knew what might await her should she lose; her life, and Jera's too, was forfeit. She had already lost her house, her husband, and her father. Now, if she lost her life, and perhaps her sister's too, she would lose *everything!*

He kicked her. She twisted her blade at him when she was pushed back, and as she pivoted, her ankle twisted, and she fell. "Gah!" she cried on the way down. Her hand swept up as the lord walked over to her, kicking the sword from her hand, clattering against the ground. It slid away, and the King's blade touched her cheek. Crushma, panting, sweat dripping from his forehead. She wanted to push herself up, but his iron boot pushed against her chest, pinning her to the ground.

"Enough of this," he panted. "There is but one way out of this. Now, where is your sister?"

"No," she grunted. "I'll not—" His foot lifted and pushed against her abdomen. The weight forced her to exhale, as her body responded to the pain inside her. "Gah! I'll not tell."

"Where is your damn sister?" he said. "I'll not ask again. This is the only way."

"No!" she said.

"Don't you understand? I am trying to save both our houses!" he hissed. "If I adopt her as my own, I can marry her off to someone that will gladly take her. Now, where is your sister?"

"Keneira!" Jera's voice cried.

She turned to where the voice came from. Her sister was there, right in front of Count Mala, whose hands grasped her sister's shoulders. A sneer was upon her face. How did she find her? Raspy breaths escaped Keneira's lips, and her heart thumped hard inside her chest. She wanted to vomit. The lord looked up, the blade of his sword still resting on her cheek.

"Well, I don't really need you now," he said, raising the sword up for an executioner's blow.

"Crushma." Mala opened her mouth. Keneira turned her head from the blade to her sister. Frightened was she, and deservedly so. There was no telling what Mala would do, not with a hostage as valuable to the lord than anything else. Was she trying to help? She was so kind last night, if a little unsettling. "I…" She took something from her pocket; Keneira couldn't tell what it was. "…had other plans."

Mala took the item, deftly brought it to Jera's throat, and suddenly red blood poured down.

"No!" Keneira cried as her sister collapsed to the ground.

The king swore, and Mala laughed. Her sister… her blood was on Mala's hands. The foot of the King released from her stomach, and she sprinted to her sister, crying. Tears rolled down her face as she tried to stop the bleeding but alas, life had already left Jera's body. Her soul had departed this disgusting world. Jera's life, and her happiness and joy, the innocence behind those eyes was the reason Keneira did anything tonight. Now, she was dead.

"You don't get to decide—"

"Keneira killed the prince, an act of treason, and yet you failed to enact your own justice!" Mala replied. "You're not fit to wear the crown."

"It was for the good of the land," Crushma sprinted at her with a drawn blade.

Mala deftly disarmed the king with her own dagger, thrusting it into his throat and twisting; his sword clattered to the ground, as lifeless as he was. The Count turned to Keneira, and she had nothing to defend herself with. What did it matter? In a single night, her attempt to save her sister from a rotten marriage only got her killed, and so too, the line of the king, and their house was destroyed. Pitted against her mentor, she had killed him. Her husband and her father… executed. And now, her sister, slain before her eyes.

"Keneira, dear," Mala said, with a sly smile on her face. "Why, oh why did you have to go and kill the lord?"

Keneira felt a rock strike her face.

CHAPTER 15

KENEIRA GROANED. WHEN SHE OPENED her
eyes, she found herself tied to the bottom of an
iron slab. Holes within it, the other end tied to
four horses. Pain seared through her face. How long
had she been unconscious? Where was she? Suddenly,
a vision flashed before her, her sister.

"Jera!" she cried. Seeing her death a second time
wasn't any easier. She had lost everything.

"You're awake," Mala's voice rang through the
air. Her dress was beautiful, but for such a person it
was ill suited. "Nice to see you again. You ready for
another grand adventure?"

"Damn you, you bitch!" she screeched. "Damn
you. I'll kill you!"

"By the Four Gods," Mala gasped. "Here I am,
doing you a favor."

"After killing my sister, your favor can go throw
itself over the wall!" she kicked against the slab to no
avail.

"You killed the king," she said. "And plunged the West into chaos."

"You did that, you treasonous bitch!"

"Well, you killed the prince," Keneira gasped with the accusation. "Since you've been unconscious, the north has quelled the invasion of the Nezkama. We're whole, yet again. We will have a summit about who will replace the king, and likely get into more petty squabbles. Not that I mind, of course," Mala sneered. "Your house and the king's house are now combined into one, and whoever is crowned king or queen, I hope yours truly, will inherit it. Why, we're practically sisters now, aren't we? Of course, your being alive complicates things, for if you were found alive, you'd be crowned, but with so many people asking for your head, you'd barely last a week." She clicked her tongue. "So that you're not surprised, I'm going to tell you what I'm going to do with you. I'm taking you to the south, selling you to a brothel. Got a nice fancy reward down there for those who used to own land, for which you very much qualify." She cackled. "You're out of my way, and you get to live. It seems a wonderful trade, if you ask me."

Keneira ground her teeth, her eyes narrowed so she could stare her hatred into Mala's eyes. She hated this count, and soon, perhaps, this lord. She was involved with one royal assassination, which was botched up so badly it cost her everything. Literally everything. Now, she was to be made into a common whore, used for some miller's breeding sow. No, there would be no breeding in her womb. Not one bit. She would bite their pricks off before they touched her!

"I will buy my freedom, Mala," she ground out. "And when I do, I'm going to raze your land to the ground."

"Well, suit yourself, and good luck!" Mala walked past her, all while cackling at Keneira's misfortune.

G L O S S A R Y

The Abyss: The Abyss is considered "no-man's land". It is a vast darkness that extends over the Land of Dreams. During the night, it encroaches closer to the lights, waiting for the light to go out, and devours any soul caught in it. It is known there are monsters inside the Abyss, and it is a caution to go off the roads or out of the cities without ample light. Due to the time that has long since passed since the Abyss first came into being, no one knows its history.

The Four Gods: The Land of Dreams adopts a poly-theistic religion which contains Four Gods of the Four Virtues: Fertility, Scars, War, and Serenity.

Land of Dreams: The long standing empire in which these four lands live. History is only recorded down for the last 1,000 years. No one knows how long the Land of Dreams has been around, nor how long the walls have been built.

Nezka: Nezka is a race of humanoid shape. They are about the same height and size of humans with the exception of horns, wings, and tails. Due to malnourishment, many of them are born with holes and tears in their wings. They have specialized clothing to account for the extra appendages. They rule the Northlands.

Nezkama: These are human/Nezka half-breeds. They are taller than their human and Nezka counterparts, but don't have wings. There are more Nezkama slaves than of the other races due to a history of racial discrimination rampant from both humans and Nezka. It is a rare occurrence that Nezkama gets along well among others, even amongst fellow slaves. These people rule the Eastlands.

Pocket: A pocket refers to any occupied territory secluded within the Abyss. Pockets do not have green orbs over them and rely heavily on Quesh'kal.

Quesh'kal: A metal mined in caverns. It is burnable material and very expensive.

A Note from the Author

You know, with as fast as I write you'd think I'd be accustomed to writing a little note as to why I write or put together this particular piece of fiction. Even now my mind isn't exactly in this book per se but my trip coming up, at the writing of this would be in a few short weeks, but perhaps months before you've picked up this book. The trip will of course be Japan and feels in some ways like a second home to me with the cultural dichotomy such as it is, is enticing to me in several ways. Not only is that country rich in history in ways no other country truly is, holding the oldest Imperial system in the world (let's hope it lasts), but also is very beautiful. One of the places I could be and I wouldn't hesitate about hopping on a train and go 100 miles from my house to see parts I've never been. Now, Japan has nothing to do with the contents of this individual book, and is quite frankly, the polar opposite of Japan!

As you can tell I'm blindly writing this here note, but I would implore you for the sake of all that is good to leave a review at your favorite aggregate. Goodreads, Amazon, and the like. The more you like this book, the more I can enjoy a nice bottle of Sake!

Kanpai!

ACKNOWLEDGEMENTS

WHAT BOOK WOULDN'T BE COMPLETE without a few. . .okay several hundred hurdles but who is counting? I want to thank the team at Miblart for the cover as they always do a good job and make changes last minute. I want to thank my editor: Belle Emanuelle who has seen several renditions of this piece. I want to thank the series of beta readers who told me what was wrong with this piece and what parts I should develop more. But as I am of the belief that books are not mere stories but histories of real persons and places in other worlds, I want to thank Keneira for putting up with me.

About the Author

K EN HARROW GREW UP IN the gritty pits of despair, he comes from: Bridgeton, Maine, a terribly dreadful place. Currently residing in the Greater Boston Area with his family, he studied Criminal Justice, English, and currently dabbles in a little bit of Finance. His unfaltering passion for writing came from his first exposure from the Lord of the Rings, which he drew inspiration from in his first stories, but alas, as all good things come downward into the grimdark pits, adopting tones from Joe Abercrombie. He loves reading, playing games of all kinds, and he is what you call a practicing writaholic. He is personally known for his witty sarcastic unasked for remarks. He works in the healthcare industry and can assure you, yes, we are listening to your calls.